LOVE AFTER

SHAY DAVIS

AUTHOR'S NOTES

Book number nine! I can't believe it! Thank you so much for rocking with me on this journey. It means a lot and I really appreciate it! As always, a huge shout out to my test readers and the entire K. Renee Presents Team! There's nothing like having a community to show continued love and support.

Please note that this is a standalone; however, Melanie was introduced in A Dash of Christmas Magic. It is not required to read that story first, but it is suggested.

Chapter One

MELANIE

"I now pronounce you husband and wife. Introducing for the first time... Mr. and Mrs. Malachi Long."

The officiant bellowed to the very small crowd of people celebrating my little brother and his new bride, also now my new best friend.

I was so happy for them. They were encased in nothing but deep love for one another. Their happily-ever-after had a few tears slipping from my lids, feeling an overwhelming amount of joy for them, but also feeling deep sorrow for my own failed marriage.

The sorrow I felt had nothing to do with the man, but rather pity for myself for being so blind all these years and staying with someone who I truly did not love, simply for complacency.

My failed attempt at happy-ever-after was all my fault.

Yeah, my husband cheated on me, and even had a baby on me. But I knew years ago that I didn't want to be with that man. And after months of sitting on my therapist's couch, it still wasn't clear as to why I stayed so long. I want to chalk it up to my daughter, Naomi, but that was probably only forty percent of the real reason. I was looking for the other sixty percent, so I could find closure. I didn't need closure from Gordon's trifling ass. However, I did need it for myself, so I wouldn't repeat any of those decisions in future relationships.

I had to shake off the direction of my thoughts. This moment wasn't about me.

It was about my handsome baby brother and his gorgeous bride.

They walked down the aisle hand in hand with huge smiles on their faces.

Photographers were in front and behind them capturing the love oozing off both of them. And even though they had professional photographers surrounding the venue and the guests, Naomi and Zinae were milling about with their cameras and drones capturing the entire scene.

The entire day was just beautiful.

The guests made their way to the other side of the huge estate Malachi rented for the reception.

The small ceremony was outside on the water. The reception took place in the huge great room that was open to a beautiful veranda with the pool and the ocean as a backdrop. It was simply breathtaking.

Malachi and Sinaa decided not to have a wedding party, which made the entire day run smoothly.

Now that the nuptials were done, I was ready to have a drink and enjoy the property.

With the party getting into full swing and the happy couple making their rounds, the dance floor opened up.

The DJ was killing it, and I couldn't keep my butt still in my seat.

Then, the melodies went from head bangers to slow and sexy.

I watched my baby brother hold his wife as they swayed to the rhythm of Eric Benét's *Real Love*. And once again, my mind was taken on an emotional rollercoaster.

I hope to look as happy as those two one day.

The way they stared at one another was what dreams were made of.

"Can I have this dance, beautiful?"

I was pulled out of my reverie by a deep, sexy baritone. One that I had not heard, or at least remembered hearing, before.

I definitely would have remembered that panty-dropping voice, I told myself.

When I looked up, this man, fitted in a perfectly tailored suit that did wonders to his broad physique, was staring down at me.

"Sure."

This was a wedding, right? I was supposed to be having fun and letting loose.

And I have never laid eyes on anyone nearly as sexy as this man--with his smooth skin, the shade of rich coffee beans, his tall stature, and commanding presence--he seemed like the perfect person to help me loosen up.

I allowed him to take my hand and lead the way to the dance floor.

We swayed to the melodic tones of Musiq Soulchild's *So Beautiful*. The way he gripped my waist and pulled me closer to him had my sleeping body awakening for the first time in years. It was as if he commanded my nerve endings to respond with just a simple touch.

I hadn't let my cheating husband touch me long before I found out about his adulterous ways, and honestly... I sealed that part of my body tight a long time ago.

But this man's hands and one dance seemed to be undoing all of that.

"You're so beautiful, Melanie. I was hoping our paths crossed today."

I was surprised that he knew my name. Because I had absolutely no idea who he was. But I was damn sure going to find out.

"I'm sorry, have we met before?" I asked curiously.

"No, we haven't. Not that I haven't tried to meet you. But Malachi told me to stay away from his *married* sister, so I was never allowed the opportunity to formally introduce myself to you."

"Hmmm," I responded, even more interested now. "I'm sorry you have me at a disadvantage... what's your name?"

"Warrick. Warrick Jones."

I was wracking my brain because I knew I heard that name somewhere. Maybe I did know this man.

"You sure we've never met? Your name sounds awfully familiar."

He let out a low chuckle that I felt rumble through his body as we were chest to chest.

"I'm sure you have heard of me. I used to play professional football for Miami. I'm retired now, but I'm on T.V. every night of football season as the host of *The War Room*."

Ahhh... I have heard of him.

"Oh, okay. Well, I have definitely heard of you, Warrick. It's a pleasure to meet you in person. I have to admit that I'm not a huge football fan, but I have seen your show a time or two when Malachi visited me in the past."

Warrick looked down at me, intrigued. I guess there weren't too many people that didn't know or cared about his celebrity status.

I inwardly shrugged and hoped like hell he wasn't about to be one of those annoying ass athletes who like to talk about themselves.

He surprised me.

Instead of talking about himself, he asked me questions.

"Can I assume, since you've been alone all night, that your husband didn't accompany you to the wedding?"

"I'm separated, actually. So, no one is here as my escort."

"That's his mistake... letting such a lovely woman slip through his fingers."

"Oh, definitely his mistake," I replied.

"Uh oh... from the sound of it, it seems like he has something coming to him."

"He definitely does. But I don't want to talk about that."

He nodded, and we continued to sway to the music. When the DJ picked it back up with some dance songs, I even turned in his arms and gave him a little booty action. Surprisingly, Warrick held my hips tight and kept up with me as I gyrated to the beat.

Warrick's hands slid along my sides, gripping my waist, all the while his hips movements behind me matched my own. The energy between us was scorching. The heat of our touch caused tingles to dance along my skin. And the moistening of my panties was making a puddling mess.

This was new to me, but I was pleased.

It seemed like we danced all night. I was truly having a great time.

When the few partygoers started to disperse, I was ready to leave and live it up for the night. With Warrick.

"Can I join you back at your hotel? I would invite you to my room, but I'm staying here on the estate."

Warrick leaned down, and his lips came deliciously close to my ear, causing shivers to travel down my spine.

"As amazing as that sounds, Melanie, I am going to have to pass. But I do hope to see you again."

I was stuck. We had been hitting it off all night. I was confused as to why he didn't want that to continue.

But I wasn't thirsty, so I smiled up at him and simply nodded.

"Well, it was nice meeting you, Warrick."

Quite frankly, I wasn't really feeling being played.

However, as I walked off, I was hoping to see him again... with his fine ass.

I walked over to my brother wishing him my last final congratulations before he and Sinaa disappeared to their wing of the estate. I'm sure I wouldn't see them before they left for their flight out to Belize early the next morning.

"I'm so happy for you, baby brother."

He hugged me tight and smiled down at me.

"Thanks, Mel," Malachi replied, kissing me on the forehead.

Even though he was my little brother. I always felt protected in his presence, and I appreciated all he did to make me feel safe after our parents passed.

"Now did I see you grinding all up on Warrick James?"

I rolled my eyes heavenward.

Just when I thought I liked his protective nature.

"Don't start, Malachi."

"Yea, leave her alone, baby." Sinaa walked up and chided Malachi.

"Thanks, Si."

She hugged me tight and said in my ear, loud enough for my brother to hear.

"I got you, boo. He's sexy as hell... do that stuff!"

"Aye... you better stop with that," Malachi reprimanded. "Seriously, Mel... he ain't the one."

"Shouldn't you be getting ready to consummate your marriage? Leave me alone."

I made quick work of saying bye to them one last time before disappearing inside, not allowing Malachi to say anything else.

It was time for me to go rest my feet and silently lick my wounds. Because I was sure I had locked in some dick for the evening.

I guess I lost my touch.

Chapter Two

MELANIE

I did not want to be back here. I hated everything the state of Tennessee represented. And the last thing I wanted was to leave the paradise of Naples, Florida, and step back into everything that reminded me of my failed marriage.

To add to that, when I got settled and pulled up my email, I had several messages from my lawyer stating that Gordon was evading service.

I don't know why he wanted to play with me. He would only end up getting his damn neck broken if I decided to call Malachi.

However, I wanted to handle my own problems and let my brother enjoy his wife.

I know how to get his ass.

I picked up the phone to call Trudy's fake Christian ass.

"Hello?"

"Trudy," I spoke dryly into the phone. "I'll make this quick. Tell your adulterous son that if he keeps evading service of my petition for divorce, I will send my process server down to the church in the middle of Sunday service and have him make a scene. And trust me, he would not mind one iota... I believe he's an atheist, so it would be his pleasure to disrupt what y'all call spreading God's word. Gordon has until Friday to accept service... don't test me, Trudy."

I hung up on her ass before she could even respond.

I hated being petty and stooping so low. But I had no choice. Gordon was forcing my hand.

Then I had to laugh at my damn self, because I had no damn clue as to the religious beliefs of the damn process server. However, it sounded good to add that little tidbit.

"Mommy, what are you laughing at?"

Naomi came and sat next to me on the couch.

"Oh, nothing."

"So, you're going crazy on me already? Aren't you like only thirty-six? It's too soon for me to be taking care of my senile mama."

"Naomi, you better get away from me, child, before I hurt you."

She laughed but left the room.

I had to shake my head at my beautiful, pain in the ass daughter. She was taking all the stuff between her dad and I really well. But I knew I raised her right, and I taught her at an early age that men are not the sole resource for happiness. And I really believed my almost sixteen-year-old daughter saw how unhappy her father was making me and felt absolutely no way about me taking back my power.

"Hey, Aunt Mel... my sister being a pain in the..."

I cut my eye at Zinae.

"Don't get cute, little girl because ya mama is off on her honeymoon."

I didn't know how the hell I was going to get through three weeks of these two girls. They were something else. And I needed to be sure that I watched my every damn move, because if I did the slightest thing, they deemed embarrassing, I would be all over their damn social media.

"Sorry," Zinae replied. "Thanks for letting me come hang out with you and Naomi. It's good to be able to spend time with her and get to see my grandparents while I'm here."

"You don't have to thank me, Nae. I wouldn't have it any other way. I love you, little girl. And I am so glad you're in mine and Naomi's lives."

Zinae hugged me tight before running off up the stairs, no doubt scheming with her sister on how to keep their eight million YouTube followers entertained.

I sat back and thought about how those two girls were the only things Gordon's grimy ass actually got right. It still amazes me how small the damn world is. Who would have thought that my no-good ass, soon-to-be ex-husband has been trifling since he was a teenager?

Gordon choosing to forgo telling me he had a daughter when we met in college was the epitome of trifling.

And my *stand-by-your-vows* ass would probably have never found out about Zinae if Sinaa hadn't met and fell in love with my brother.

But I was glad to have Zinae and Sinaa in my life now. And I loved the bond Naomi was building with her newfound sister. It made my heart swell to be able to witness the immediate bond between them.

Chapter Three

MELANIE

"Melanie! I missed you, girl!"

Sinaa ran up to me and held me tight when I walked into the new house my brother purchased for them.

I had to admit that I was loving all the back-and-forth travel to Florida. I loved it here, so it didn't bother me one bit to hop on these flights. Especially when Malachi was footing the bill.

"I mean, damn... it's only been three weeks, Si."

She laughed.

"And my ass couldn't wait to get back so my coochie could rest. Ya brother has been fucking my brains out every single chance he got."

"Umm... ILL!"

"What? Don't girlfriends normally talk about this stuff? I'm not sure... I haven't had many, or shit to really talk about when it came to men."

This girl!

"Yes, I suppose this is stuff that girlfriends talk about, but he's still my brother, so I'm going to need you to be mindful of that. I don't particularly want to know how he be diggin' you out."

The dreamy look that crossed her mind had me laughing. I knew at that exact moment that I had better get my ears ready for hearing way too much shit about my brother's sex life.

"Well, shit... can you sprinkle a little of that juju on me, because I need someone to come pull all the honey out of my flower?"

"Really, Mel? Are you really using a bee analogy?"

I shrugged.

"Well, bees pull the honey out so damn well. I need a man to imitate that and make shit happen between my thighs. Bring some life back to my pussy."

"Definitely a conversation worthy of our YouTube channel."

Both Sinaa and I turned and looked up at the top of the steps.

"Y'all better stay y'all asses out of grown folks' business. And so help me God... if I see this *private* conversation posted on social media, I'm shutting all that shit down."

I've never actually threatened to really shut them down, but I meant every word I said. Naomi and Zinae were going a little too far and too grown with this one.

"Yes, ma'am," they responded in unison and walked off.

"Girl, let's go grab something to eat before you kill them both," Sinaa said, laughing.

"Yes, and maybe I'll see some fine ass chocolate men out and about."

"Yea, let's get your honeypot tended to."

"Yes, let's."

We ended up dining at Amara at Paraiso. It was right on the

water, and while it had all the Miami feels, it wasn't directly on Miami beach with all the extra that came along with dining there.

"So, apart from the sex, how was your honeymoon?"

"Girl, it was amazing. Belize is so beautiful. I told Malachi that I wanted a vacation home there. He started looking at real estate that night, so I'm expecting it as a birthday gift or something. You know how your brother is with, *wanting to give me the world*."

I swooned. Love looked so good on them. And I knew my brother was good for it, so I wouldn't be surprised if he gifted Sinaa with a beautiful beachfront property on the coast of Belize. And my ass would be right there every vacation season.

"I'm so happy you two found one another. I was sure Malachi was going to be fucking bitches in his beachfront condo forever."

"Aht aht. I don't wanna hear about them hoes!"

I laughed so loud, I drew attention to our table.

"It doesn't matter. He only has eyes for his wife now."

"Zackly," Sinaa said in her ghetto girl voice, that absolutely did not fit her. "And that's why his ass sold that damn condo too!"

I laughed even harder at that. Sinaa was not playing with my brother. And I was here for it all.

"I knew I heard that beautiful laugh. I had to come and investigate."

I turned to see who was trying to spit wack ass lines, but was met with the sexy smile and gaze that belonged to none other than Warrick Jones.

Chapter Four

WARRICK

I sat at the bar enjoying an Old Fashioned when I heard *that* laugh. I knew immediately who it belonged to. And I was surprised to hear it.

I knew Melanie lived in Tennessee, and I would have thought she'd gone back by now. Her brother's wedding was a few weeks ago.

However, my body knew the moment it was assaulted by that melodic sound that she was in fact still in Florida, and still had an influence over my body.

It was so damn hard to turn her down that night. But I really didn't want to fight with Malachi over his sister. And I knew that he would not be okay with me taking her back to my hotel room.

Also, I don't think she had any idea what she was really asking for. I was one hundred percent certain that she was not ready for the likes of Warrick Jones.

"Warrick," Melanie said breathlessly.

I smirked down at her, realizing I was having the same effect on her that she was having on me.

"It's a pleasure running into you again, Melanie."

Then it was as if she remembered I declined her offer to extend our night together, because her face frowned up.

"I cannot say the same."

I chuckled.

"Fair enough. I'll let you two get back to your lunch. Sinaa," I turned to her, "Congratulations again on your nuptials. It was a beautiful ceremony."

"Thank you, Warrick. I'll be sure to tell Malachi I ran into you and extend your well wishes to him as well."

I caught what she was saying, between the lines."

I'm going to tell my husband you are checking for his sister. That's what she was really telling me.

All I could do was nod, letting her know that I understood.

"Well, ladies... I won't keep you."

Neither of them replied, but before I was completely out of earshot, I heard Sinaa saying, *ohhh... I'm gonna tell your brother.* And then they both fell out into a fit of giggles, allowing me to bask in the beautiful sounds that escaped Melanie's throat.

I walked off with thoughts of Melanie on my mind. I knew she was forbidden fruit, but damn if she didn't look so appealing.

I needed to get my thoughts and dick in order, because the last thing I wanted to do was cause a rift with Malachi. He and I had become great friends over the years, and I truly appreciated his friendship.

However, I could not stop my thoughts traveling back to Melanie, and her long and smooth curvy legs, wild bouncy hair, full lips, and beautiful deep mahogany complexion.

I wanted her, and bad.

After an amazing trip back to Florida, Naomi and I were back home and back to our regular routines.

It was summer, and Naomi was signed up for a cinematography summer program, so my days were spent home alone in the huge house that held nothing but emptiness for me.

It was moments like this when I wished I wouldn't have given up my career for Gordon's no-good ass. But I did have a college education in African American History, and I contemplated going back to teaching in a classroom.

I had truly missed it, even though it had been over ten years since I taught in a school.

No time like the present to reinvent yourself.

With Gordon finally accepting service and my attorney working on a marital settlement agreement, I was ready to move on to the next phase in life.

Hopefully, that phase held a big black dick and endless nights of mindless, pleasurable sex.

I needed it.

Thinking of getting laid had my honeypot twitching and thoughts of Warrick combing their way to the surface of my brain. I tried so hard to put him out of my mind, but his body was simply a masterpiece that could not be forgotten.

Warrick looked like the type of man that could pick me up and fuck me right on whatever surface he deemed formidable.

It was only ten in the morning, but the heat traveling through my body from thoughts of Warrick's large frame surrounding mine and bringing me to heights my body has never known, caused me to need a drink.

I went into the kitchen and made myself the biggest mimosa. I figured that was a drink appropriate for this early in the morning, so I indulged, not feeling a bit of shame.

Getting comfortable at the island with my laptop, I began to research teaching jobs in Tennessee and Florida.

Nothing really held me here any longer. So, the thoughts of being closer to my brother and new sister-in-law, looked real satisfying. Naomi would also get the chance to spend time with her sister and build on their ever-growing relationship.

Looking down at my phone buzzing on the countertop, I rolled my eyes and sincerely debated on sending the shit to voicemail, but against my better judgment, I picked up.

"What do you want?"

"I am not giving you the house, Melanie! And I am definitely not giving you half of my 401(k). Have you lost your damn mind?!"

I sighed into the phone over Gordon's weak ass voice coming through the speakerphone.

"Fine, Gordon. Don't sign the agreement. We will see what a judge has to say. My lawyer said I was being quite liberal, so let's leave it up to a judge then. However, I have better shit to do with my life, so good day."

"You bitch! You don't have shit to do besides be lazy and leech off me. I pay the damn bills in that house. If I stopped paying today, your ass will be out on the street in two months because I know you can't afford the mortgage."

I tuned his ass out while he ranted and raved, because little did he know, I have been taking money from our savings account for the past five years. His stupid ass never even noticed.

"Then stop paying the mortgage then, Gordon. Go ahead and put your daughter out on the street. I wouldn't be surprised... your track record with your children is shitty. I hope your new baby mama knows she probably only got a few good years before you throw her and her daughter out like trash. It's what you do best. Discard what's supposed to be top priority. And that is because you are a pussy ass muthafucka without a backbone, raised by a pussy ass momma and daddy. So, do what you want. Good day, Gordon."

I didn't even let his ass get another word in. I hung up on that little weasel ass bitch.

I wanted to bang my head against the counter, to punish myself for ever being so dumb as to allow him to feed me lies and bullshit for so long.

Not anymore! I was done. And since Gordon wanted a fight, I planned on dusting off my Timbs and getting the Vaseline ready. Gordon's ass didn't really know Mel from them BK streets. He ain't want war, but since he wanted to play... that's what his ass was going to get.

I was ready to go find my gangsta rap playlist and get my mind right.

I let out a loud chuckle because I was really thinking the most.

Once I finally settled my little inner hood rat, who's been repressed for damn near two decades, I picked up my phone to call my lawyer.

"Hello?"

"Hi Vanessa, it's Melanie. I just got a call from my no-good-ass, soon-to-be ex, and he's claiming he wants a fight."

"I figured as much when I received his answer to our complaint. He's denying all claims, and has filed a counter-complaint. I was actually going to email you today."

"Figures. I'm ready for war."

Vanessa chuckled.

"Calm down, killa. I may still be able to talk him down through his attorney. Give me a few weeks to see what I can come up with. In the meantime, send me over all your financials, and any documentation regarding the allegations he is denying and claiming in his countersuit."

"I already have everything scanned in and separated. You'll have everything by the end of the day."

"Sounds good. I love it when the opposing side chooses to be a dick, and I have a chance to stick it to them."

"Shit, with your hourly rate, you better."

"Hey! You're getting the family discount thanks to Sinaa, so don't go lawyer-bashing!"

We both laughed at that.

"For real, Vanessa, thank you for all that you're doing. I really do appreciate it."

"No problem. Girl power! Let's take his ass to the bank."

Now that's what I like to hear.

Vanessa and I talked a few moments more about strategy, and I had to admit, I was kind of happy Gordon took the hard way out. It would feel good taking every possible dime I could from his pockets.

Fuck him.

Chapter Six

MELANIE

"Melanie Brown v. Gordon Brown… are all parties present?"

"The Plaintiff is present, Your Honor," Vanessa responded to the female judge.

The man I assumed was Gordon's attorney, looked all around the courtroom as if Gordon's butt was going to appear out of thin air.

"Your Honor, I am still waiting for my client."

"Mr. Namen, did your client not receive proper notice of the hearing?"

"He did, Your Honor. He just called and said he's stuck in traffic and should be arriving momentarily."

I wanted to suck my teeth. There wasn't any damn traffic in this small ass town. His ass is just doing what he normally does… disregarding anyone but himself.

Vanessa cut her eye at me as if warning me to keep my thoughts to myself.

I nodded and took a deep breath. I refused to be baited into stepping out of character today.

I only wanted to get today over with. The last few months were beyond stressful, fighting with Gordon over every little dollar. He really tried to make my life miserable and acted as if I was the one who committed adultery.

Finally, Gordon came rushing through the doors of the courtroom.

"Sorry, Your Honor."

"Mr. Brown, please have a seat. I do not take kindly to my time being wasted."

A little smile did escape my lips. Gordon was already pissing the judge off, and I didn't mind.

"Before we begin, I see there's an outstanding motion. Mr. Namen, your client is asking that Ms. Spelling be barred from representing Mrs. Brown... on what grounds, counsel?"

"Ms. Spelling works with the mother of Mr. Brown's first child, and we are arguing that it's a conflict of interest. The two women, well three, if you include Ms. Spelling, are teaming up to punish my client beyond what is deemed reasonable in this action."

"Your Honor, if I could?" The judge nodded at Vanessa. "The mother of the Defendant's child does not work at the Clarington location. She, in fact, practices in our New York offices, only ever coming into the office when she's in town for extended holiday stays. Even then, she works remotely on her current caseload. She very rarely provides counsel on actual cases taking place in our office. Thus, this motion is absurd, and reaching. The Defendant is simply trying to extend litigation, which would be to his benefit, because he has already attempted to move funds around."

"Let me get this straight, Mr. Namen. You are saying that counsel for the Plaintiff is not able to represent Mrs. Brown because of an attorney who doesn't even practice here in Clarington? And if I were you, I would be careful with my words, because you are essentially claiming that Ms. Spelling is being unethical and putting her license on the line."

My focus was bouncing between the judge, Vanessa, and Gordon's obvious incompetent attorney.

"Well... I... I..."

His ass was stuttering something fierce.

"I'm simply saying that the facts could be skewed by the degrees of separation."

"Motion denied, counselor."

That's what his ass gets.

I couldn't believe he really tried to stoop so low as to get my lawyer thrown off my damn case.

Asshole!

"Ms. Spelling, are you ready for your opening?"

"Yes, Your Honor."

Vanessa stood up, walked in front of our table, and spoke in a loud, commanding voice.

"Your Honor, this case is quite simple. As a matter of fact, it could have been settled outside of this courtroom today, and allowed the court to focus on more serious matters. My client, Melanie Brown, has been with the Defendant for approximately sixteen years. Most of which he was not around for. However, Mrs. Brown stood valiantly by her husband's side and raised their daughter. After years of being hidden away from the people closest to him, Mrs. Brown found out that the Defendant had fathered a child outside of their marriage, and found out about an older child that he hid from my client. The Defendant's youngest child and her mother are in fact living with and being taken care of by the Defendant's parents, right here in Clarington, under Mrs. Brown's nose.

Even with all the recent betrayals of her husband, Mrs. Brown simply wants to disassociate herself from the Defendant, and asks the court to award a fair and equitable distribution of the parties' assets. Mrs. Brown put her career on hold to help the Defendant advance his own career, and to care for their daughter. Neither of which Mrs. Brown objected to. She loved her husband and wanted to be there as his wife, providing whatever support he needed. However, after years of putting her own needs aside, Mrs. Brown believes she deserves a fair share of everything she helped the Defendant obtain over the last sixteen years. That is all, Your Honor. Thank you for your time today."

Vanessa kept it super classy while still pointing out how shitty Gordon's ass has been. And I appreciated it. I really didn't want this entire situation to turn into a knockdown, drag-out fight. I really just wanted what I deserved of all of the money Gordon made over the years, sell our house, and move the hell on.

I really didn't understand why he was trying not to give me any damn thing. The way his mind worked was ridiculous. He ignored Naomi and me for years, hid a child, and created another child with another woman.

Like, why the hell did he think that he was going to walk away with all his assets? That muthafucka was crazy for real. And he really was going to make me take it back to my much younger hood days if he kept playing.

Gordon gonna fuck around and find sugar in his gas tank and four flat tires.

I literally zoned out the entire time Gordon's lawyer went

through his opening... I wouldn't be able to repeat not one word he spoke. But honestly, I didn't give a damn. I've never done one negative thing to my husband during our entire marriage. For some God-forsaken reason, I stood idle by his side, supporting his every damn move against my brother's wishes.

So, his lawyer could say whatever the hell he wanted.

As the trial progressed, Gordon tried to lie about balances in his bank accounts, retirement accounts, and even tried to leave a few accounts out of evidence.

However, while I was a stay-at-home mom, I was the fuck far from dumb. I had copies of everything and already provided them to Vanessa.

Gordon trying to lie about, or smooth talk around details, turned the judge off. She stopped him several times while he was on the stand testifying, reminding him that he was under oath.

Him and his attorney were just a damn joke, and the judge saw right through their acts.

After hours and hours of testifying and submitting documents into evidence for the judge to review, closing statements were presented. We were told we could break and be back in the courtroom at four-thirty for her ruling.

Vanessa and I left the courthouse and went to a coffee shop across the street, both needing some caffeine after the trying day.

"You did good, Mel. I'm proud of you. You decided to go high every time you could've gone low during cross-examination."

"Okay, lil' Michelle Obama. *When they go low, we go high,*" I mocked.

We both fell out into laughter.

"But seriously, there were a few times I really wanted to

throw jabs. But you know what, Vanessa? What I want more than anything is for this to be over. I'm just drained. I'm ready to be free from Gordon. Between finding out about his new baby, and the fact that he deserted Zinae... I simply could not justify finally putting an end to our dead-end situation. If I would have stayed, what image would I be portraying to my daughter? How would that have made Zinae feel since she's been in my life recently just as much as my own daughter? I wouldn't be able to take in my own reflection if I didn't finally decide that mine and Gordon's marriage has gone on for far too long."

I was a little emotional once I finished talking. As much as I was ready for my marriage to be over, it was still a part of my life that needed mourning. If I were honest with myself, I probably waited so damn long to take this step because I didn't think I had it in me to mourn anything else in my life.

Getting with Gordon dulled the mourning of my parent's death. Now that I wouldn't have this dead-end situation as my little metaphoric blanky, I would be forced to feel the effects of my failed marriage, and everything else I buried for the past decade and a half.

Vanessa reached her hand across the table and pulled my hand in hers, giving me a supportive squeeze.

"You're doing the right thing, Melanie. Your strength is definitely empowering. I see women hold off filing for divorce every day simply because they think it's going to be too hard. You deserve to be happy."

I smiled back at her, thanking her for her support.

"And from the vibes I'm getting from the judge, you're going to have a great nest egg to lay down as a foundation in finding what makes you happy."

I laughed.

"Well, shit! Let's get our asses back over to the courthouse so I can go collect my funds."

We got up and walked out of the coffee shop full of giggles.

Vanessa was worth every penny Malachi was paying her. She was also shaping up to be a great friend.

———

"All rise!"

The bailiff's voice boomed through the courtroom after we were all settled back in.

I wasn't sure why I was nervous, but I was just buzzing with energy that had me sweating. The way my armpits were perspiring under my suit jacket had me thinking about if I remembered to put deodorant on before I left the house.

The judge stepped up to her bench from her chambers and took a seat.

"You may all be seated."

She pulled her little specs on her face and ruffled through her papers before speaking again.

I wanted to shout, *didn't you just look over those damn documents? Get to it.*

Because now all I could think about was my armpits and the possibility of smelling like an old hoagie.

Yeah, ya ass is crazy nervous.

My internal dialog was driving me even crazier. I think it was because the end was so close that I could taste it, whether I got half of everything or not.

"I've reached my decision. Everything I state here will be drafted in a final Judgement of Absolute Divorce, and original copies will be given to counsel for the parties."

If she doesn't get on with this shit.

I couldn't stop shaking my leg under the table. It felt like I was running a race, and the closer the finish line entered my sight, it seemed to move back a few more yards.

"Mr. Gordon, you're lucky I don't throw you in jail for sitting on my stand and lying under oath. But I'm feeling generous today. You are hereby ordered to pay Mrs. Brown two hundred and fifty thousand dollars, which equates to approximately fifty-five percent of your combined account, including the accounts you attempted to hide. You are also ordered to pay Mrs. Brown's attorney's fees. In addition, you are ordered to liquidate half of your retirement assets to Mrs. Brown.

As you have several individual accounts, again which you attempted to hide from the court, Mrs. Brown will have the authority with this order to remove your name from all joint accounts. Mr. Brown, you will not touch any funds in any of those joint accounts prior to having your name removed, or else I will hold you in contempt of court and lock you up.

Mrs. Brown, you will retain ownership of the marital residence. You will have all that you need in my executed order to remove Mr. Brown from the deed and mortgage. I am granting you sole physical and legal custody of your daughter, with the proposed visitation schedule submitted by your attorney. Mr. Brown, you also ordered to pay two thousand six-hundred dollars, monthly, in child support. Finally, Mrs. Brown, I am approving your request to return to your maiden name of Melanie Erica Long."

The judge banged her gavel one last time.

"Court adjourned."

I was the hell stuck. I couldn't move.

That judge just ordered triple of what I asked for. I had to keep my damn mouth from hitting the ground.

Vanessa leaned over and whispered in my ear.

"Congratulations, Ms. Long."

I couldn't even form a response.

Chapter Seven

MELANIE

Everything with Gordon had been finalized. His name was removed from the house and our accounts, and his ass had already missed out on every scheduled weekend he was supposed to have with Naomi.

Naomi didn't care, though. She was a bright and mature young girl, and she saw her father for who he really was.

Even though she was able to have that discernment, it really did break my heart that Gordon didn't try harder to be the father she needed. Because the fact was, every girl needs her dad.

Thankfully, Naomi had Malachi. So, it only made sense that I move to Miami to be closer to him. After putting the house on the market, it sold in a blink of an eye. I was able to coax Malachi into coming to help me pack up. Well, he hired movers, but that worked for me too.

Right now, I was just thinking about the need to move in with my brother and his new wife.

Lord only knew of the therapy I was going to need after spending time in the house with them fucking like rabbits.

I let out a giggle and shook my head.

I was pulled out of my thoughts when Malachi strolled into the living room.

"So, I drove out here to move all this shit by myself and watch you drink wine in the middle of the damn day?"

"Ugh! Why do you have to be so damn extra? You're not even moving anything. You're just here because you didn't want me alone in a house full of movers."

"What kind of man would I be if I let you deal with this shit alone? Oh wait, I'd be Gordon."

I couldn't stop the laugh falling from my lips if I wanted to. My brother was a damn fool.

"Khi, I can't stand your ass. You know that?"

"But you love me, though. That's all that matters. You ready for this drive tomorrow?"

I nodded.

"As ready as I'll ever be. I'm just ready to be away from here. I never had any family or real friends here. And now that I closed the chapter of Gordon's nonsense, I'm ready to be closer to you. We haven't been in the same state since I went off to college. And I want Naomi and Zinae to be as close as possible. They are two very smart young women, and I think they can take the world by storm, separately, but definitely together."

Malachi wrapped his arms around me.

"I got you, sis... both me and Sinaa. We're going to all be good."

I burrowed into my brother and let a few tears fall. I was supposed to be older, but he always seemed to have it together. He also knew exactly what I needed when I was down. Malachi was always there to supply me with jokes and loving hugs, making me feel better.

Even though Malachi was only thirteen when our parents died, they did an amazing job instilling in him the notion that he was to protect me at all times, even though I was older. His natural, loving nature always reminded me of our parents, which always made me happy and sad.

"Don't cry, sis. Everything is going to be okay."

"I know. But I still can't help but to look at my life and think mommy and daddy would have been so disappointed. And then I look at you, and I'm so proud of you, and I know they would be proud too. I feel like such a failure."

He hugged me tighter.

"Man, will you chill with that. You are not a failure, Mel. And mom and dad would be proud of all that you went through and still came out on the other end whole."

"But am I whole? I'm not so sure."

As much as I wanted to get rid of Gordon, I didn't quite know what life meant for me next. I normally try to be optimistic, but life wasn't looking so great for me at thirty-eight.

"Shit, you're whole now! You got rid of that extra baggage, sucking the life out of you. I promise, sis... this next phase of your life is going to take you by surprise, and you're gonna love it.

"I'll take your word for it. Now, are you going to help me finish packing some of this stuff?"

"Hell, naw! I'm just here to make sure you don't get robbed, or worse, by a group of strange men. Pass me that glass and finish ya damn work."

I cackled as Malachi seriously took my wine glass from my hand, leaned against the window and watched me as I started wrapping and packing away pictures and other little knickknacks that I was going to take with me on our long drive back to Miami.

"Wait 'til I tell Sinaa how lazy you were."

"Shit, I gotta be your therapist and your maid? I think that's abuse. We should tell Sinaa that."

I shook my head at this fool.

However, I was thankful that he was here. I was even more thankful that I sent Naomi to Florida already, so that she wouldn't have to see my random bouts of tears.

Getting serious again, Malachi spoke from across the room.

"You're gonna be okay, Mel."

Water pooled in my eyes, and I nodded, praying he was right.

I was closing the Tennessee chapter of my life, and I never wanted to revisit it.

My plans were to dive in the deep end of whatever came next in my life.

Chapter Eight

WARRICK

"My man, Malachi! What's going on? I hear you have a house full of women driving you crazy."

I was really trying to get info on Melanie without getting the twenty-one questions and protective brother talk from Malachi.

"Yeah, man. My sister's divorce is finally done, and she moved here to be closer to me and the rest of the fam."

"That's what's up. Family life is suiting you well. I don't recall ever seeing you this happy."

"Thanks, War. I can't believe I have a wife and a damn teenage daughter. I'm thrust straight into scaring niggas off with my gun."

I laughed at him because I knew that feeling all too well.

"I'm sorry to say that it doesn't get better. My daughters are about to be eighteen, and them and their little so-called *boyfriends* drive me the hell crazy. When one of them little ninjas come to take Mea or Mya out on a date, I take them in the media room and watch old footage of my games. You should see their faces when I tell them my number, and they watch me tackle mofos."

Malachi's loud laughter rang out in the bar.

"War, you wrong as hell for that!"

"Shit. Mea and Mya come home every time five to ten minutes before their curfew. Them little ninjas know not to play with me."

"Man, I'm in real estate... I ain't got nothing to scare these little boys with except my fire power."

"Uh... did you forget you played ball too? You were a beast. Pull up some of those tapes... I bet it works."

Malachi and I shared more laughs over a few drinks. It was good running into him. We were always close, but currently, a part of me wanted to keep him even closer because I wanted his sister.

Malachi didn't even know he was going to be an instrumental element in me getting what I wanted.

To drive my intentions home, I invited Malachi to bring the entire family to my house for a cookout.

"That sounds cool. Zinae and Naomi are both new to town, so they'd probably enjoy meeting new people. As long as you tell Mea and Mya to keep their little male friends from my daughter and niece."

I chuckled.

"Shiddd. Maybe I'll have them send them all your way and take the headaches off my hands."

Malachi shot me a look and shook his head. He knew I was bullshitting.

We ended up kicking it for a few more hours, talking about sports and an array of different shit. Malachi finally said he had to get back to his wife.

I couldn't say that I had the desire to know that feeling. I was in control of everything in my life and liked to keep it that way.

———

My plan worked like a charm.

Well, not really, but it still worked.

Instead of Malachi bringing his family to the house, he called me and said he decided to throw something for Melanie and his niece. An, *I'm glad you're here,* type of thing.

So, he called and invited me and my girls.

I walked into the big backyard and was proud to see all that Malachi had accomplished. I was disappointed when he came to me and said football wasn't his passion and he wouldn't be entering in the draft. However, I was proud that he had an alternate plan and wanted to go into business for himself. I admired his go-getter spirit.

"Warrick, I'm glad you could make it."

"Yeah, a chance to have Mea and Mya hanging out with girls instead of boys... I'm there."

"Daddy!"

Malachi laughed.

"Good to see y'all again. My daughter Zinae and my niece Naomi are over by the pool. And it's food on the other side of the yard."

"Thank you, Mr. Malachi," they said in that freaky twin unison thing.

I followed their movements to see if they would be shy about going to introduce themselves. I guess I needed to stop looking after them as if they were my little girls and accept that they were seventeen, because they walked right up to the edge of the pool and jumped in.

Seeing them make themselves comfortable was all I needed to relax.

"You want a beer or something?" Malachi asked.

"Yeah, I'll take a beer."

I followed Malachi deeper into the backyard, and had to slow down and tell my dick to keep his shit straight. Because Melanie was over by the outdoor grill area in a high-waisted two piece.

And she was simply beautiful.

Her curves were on full display, and her breasts were spilling from her bathing suit top.

All I wanted to do was devour her luscious mahogany skin.

I strolled over to her and Sinaa, and made my presence known.

"Good afternoon, ladies."

Sinaa, as always, greeted me with a big smile and a warm sisterly hug.

Melanie stood off to the side, acting shy. But once Sinaa let me go, she nodded her head in my direction.

"Hi, Warrick. It's nice to see you again."

"You too."

All I could think about was how her body felt in mine that night on the dance floor.

Right now, I was kicking myself, because I could have known exactly how soft her skin was, everywhere. But I chose to be the ever gentleman, and repress the thoughts of me licking her body as she was tied to my bed.

My dick was really getting away from me. Even with the warning I gave, he was growing, and pointing into the direction of Melanie as if she were a beacon that had everything he needed.

Malachi appeared at my side with a beer and looked between Melanie and me.

The tension was unmistakable.

"Nahhh, War! Not my sister. She's off limits."

"Um, excuse me... did you forget that I'm grown?"

Malachi ignored her and focused on me.

We exchanged a look, and I already knew where his head was at.

He knew about my lifestyle.

"Nah, my G—not my sister," he stated again, emphatically.

I didn't respond because I knew I wasn't going to heed his warning.

I tried.

But the glow in her skin called to me. I wanted to know if her radiant, chocolate skin would turn red under my palm.

My fingers twitched with the thought of spanking her. I wanted my hands to make contact with her ass. I wanted to slap her on the pussy so good that she'd come on contact.

I wanted her to beg more for more; to own her body.

I had to walk away from her before I started World War III with her brother.

That had to be avoided at all costs. I would need to be strategic about getting Melanie in my bed.

Deciding on a chair by the pool, I looked on as Mea and Mya were making friends with Naomi and Zinae.

Switching mental gears, I was glad to see them getting along with other girls. They both always claimed to have problems with their female classmates, and I was tired of their boy-obsessed ways. I knew it had everything to do with their damn mom, but I tried not to think about that too much, because it always caused my temper to flare.

That girl wasn't nothing but a hoe. Personally, I would have thought she would have grown out of that, but no. She was still running around trapping niggas—just as she did me.

I loved my girls, but if it was one thing I regretted doing, it was trying some normal shit outside of my ordinary routine when I entered the league.

Trying to prove to myself that I could get over my childhood trauma, and actually love someone, and in turn receive true love, was the biggest mistake of my career.

All I was to women was a walking dollar sign, which is exactly what I was to Milan. Her name should have been enough to ward me off. Who the hell fucks with a girl from the hood named after a country she didn't even know existed?

But regardless, here I was, a box of tampered Magnums, and seventeen years later with tall, beautiful twin girls that looked just like their mother.

"Why do you look so forlorn?"

Melanie sat in the lounge chair next to me and handed me another beer, taking the empty one from my hand.

Already serving her Dom. I like that shit.

Malachi was really going to fuck my ass up. I already knew it.

"Nothing. Just got stuck in my head, thinking about the girls' mother."

"Oh. Well, I definitely know all about relationship fuck ups."

I chuckled.

"Yeah, Malachi told me you were newly divorced."

"Yup! Approaching forty and trying to figure out life. I'm such a lame."

"Nah. You're beautiful, and you're doing what Auntie Maxine

told you to do... reclaiming your time. Nothing wrong with that."

She let out a soft giggle, and the sound went straight to my dick.

"I guess you're right. I guess I had finally gotten enough of being used and cheated on."

"Damn. What man in their right mind would cheat on a woman as beautiful as you? He had to be out his damn mind."

"The same man that fathered Sinaa's daughter and hid her from me and the rest of the world."

My neck snapped to look at her to make sure I heard her right.

"Yup! Long ass story."

"That's crazy."

"Who you telling. Last Christmas was something else, but I got an amazing sister out of the madness."

"Family over everything. I like that."

Now it was her turn to study me. I'm not sure what about my statement made her look at me as if she were examining me under a microscope, but watching her big, pouty lips perse was fine by me.

"I think I like you, Warrick."

I smiled back at her.

"I think I like you too."

"Everybody, come eat!" Sinaa yelled out into the yard, breaking the stare-down Melanie and I had going on.

I was thankful for the distraction, because that tension was building between us again, and it was intense as hell.

You should really leave her alone, War.

Chapter Nine

MELANIE

Florida was amazing. The sunny weather, the hustle, and bustle of Miami Beach, even though Malachi and Sinaa lived about twenty-five minutes from South Beach.

The entire scene was invigorating. I was motivated to get everything out of life that I missed out on in that awful town of Clarington.

First thing was finding a teaching job. My goal was to get an adjunct position at one of the colleges, but I'd settle for a high school teaching position in the meantime.

And I had two interviews scheduled. One of which was at the girl's new private school.

That would be interesting if I secured that position. I purposely didn't tell the girls because I can only imagine the scheming they would do to keep me from getting the job.

I secretly hoped to get the position just so I can mess with them as they are always harassing everyone around them.

For now, with adjusting to everything around me, I was

looking forward to stepping out for a bit with Sinaa and getting a drink.

"What you in here laughing about, girl?"

"The girls' face if I get this job at their school."

"Mel, you don't know how much I'm praying that you get that job. We need some damn leverage with them."

I giggled, but I couldn't agree more.

"You ready to hit these streets? I found a nice lil' grown and sexy lounge off the beaten path. We should be clear from all those mumbling ass kids."

"Now that's what I'm talking about, sis. Cause I can't take that shit. I'm trying to have some nice views of grown and sexy eye candy tonight," I told Sinaa.

"Let me find out you tryna take something home."

"Well, not to this damn house, because my brother be doing the most. But I mean, he can reserve a nice hotel suite and blow my back out."

It sounded good, but I didn't think I was really ready for all of that.

"You are a mess! You're ready for that?" Sinaa asked, pulling the thoughts straight from my head.

"I don't know. I think so... maybe."

"Well, we're about to find the hell out. Let's go!" Sinaa stood and stared seriously into my eyes before she proceeded to the door of the room. "But you know you don't have to rush anything, right?"

I nodded. Silently thanking her for her support.

———

At the lounge, the crowd buzzed with the grown and sexy. And the men... they were mouthwatering. I mean, each and every one of them looked delicious.

"What can I get for you two ladies?" The bartender strolled up to us and asked.

"Can I get a tequila and sparkling water with lemon?"

"Melanie, what that fuck is that?"

"What? It's less calories. I need to get my single body back. I can't be drinking all that sugar."

Sinaa rolled her eyes at me.

"Sir, can you get me tequila... hold that damn sparkling water?"

The bartender chuckled at Sinaa and turned to wink at me. I'm sure he would have winked at Sinaa too, but she was blinding everyone with that big ass rock and three-sixty sparkling wedding band on her finger.

"Girl, you know you're scaring all my damn prospects away with that big ass rock, right? My brother is so damn extra."

Sinaa laughed so loud it reverberated over the music.

After a few drinks and some good music, Sinaa and I found ourselves out on the dance floor winding to the reggaeton beats. Just as before, men stayed away from Sinaa. But they all floated to me, trying to get my attention. However, they were all too thirsty, so I ignored them.

There was a sexy man sitting at the bar, looking absolutely delectable. I watched him watch me, but he never approached me.

I told Sinaa to order another round of drinks while I went to the lady's room. When I came out, and walked down the long corridor, the man from the bar was also coming out of the men's room.

We bumped into one another, on purpose... because we were both checking for one another.

"Excuse me, beautiful," he said.

"You're excused, handsome," I retorted, smirking.

He smiled back.

"I've been checking you for a minute, unable to look away due to that bright light that seems to surround you."

Thankfully my skin was too dark to reveal my blush.

The mystery man led us back to the main club area, which I was thankful for because it was a little creepy to be sneaking about in dark halls with a stranger.

"Mel, who's your friend?" Sinaa asked

"Not sure. I didn't catch his name," I smiled at her and responded.

"I'm Anthony."

"Nice to meet you, Anthony. I'm Sinaa, and this is my sister-in-law, Melanie."

"Well, it's nice to meet you two beautiful ladies."

Sinaa turned back to the bar and buried her face in her cell, leaving me and Anthony to talk.

Our conversation was difficult over the music, but we managed. He was a nice guy, and his tall frame, caramel skin, and waves helped with the words I couldn't quite make out, because his ass was gorgeous.

Anthony leaned down to whisper in my ear, and his minty breath tickled my senses.

"What do you say we get out of here?" He asked.

I was about to answer when a deep voice awakened every cell in my body. While Anthony was good-looking, and I was truly interested in him, the deep voice that creeped up on me controlled my body's response, against my wishes.

"Sinaa. Melanie. It's time to go."

I turned and met Warrick's gaze. The look on his face and the inflection of his tone, left nothing up for discussion.

Sinaa looked at me and shrugged her shoulders, probably thinking Malachi must have sent him for us, so she got up from her seat.

"Sinaa, you go ahead. I think I'm going to kick it with Anthony a little longer."

At my words, I felt Anthony encircle his arm around my waist, but he must've seen something in Warrick's eyes, because it dropped merely seconds after making contact.

"I'm taking both of y'all home. Let's go."

Again, nothing about his words were debatable.

Sinaa turned to me with wide eyes and mouthed, *let's go.*

I inhaled and turned to Anthony to say goodnight.

"Can I get your number before you leave?"

I looked back to see Warrick already walking away and Sinaa starting to follow behind him. I quickly typed my number in Anthony's phone and told him it was nice to meet him.

What the fuck is happening right now?

Warrick turned to look at me, and his stare seem to permeate straight to my core.

Did Malachi send him? I had to ask myself.

And if he did, why did Warrick seem to have a problem with me?

It was all too much to work through with all the tequila in my system. But I would find out.

Chapter Ten

WARRICK

I was angry as hell, and I wasn't exactly sure why.

Walking into the lounge, I spotted Sinaa sitting at the bar alone, so I figured Malachi was somewhere around. Midway in my approach, I saw Melanie come from the side corridor with a man.

My blood immediately began to boil.

Why the fuck is she coming from the bathroom with a nigga?

I slowed my pace to further survey the scene in front of me. I wanted to know how familiar ole boy was with what was mine.

Because Melanie *was* mine.

It only took one dance, or a night of dancing rather, to confirm that fact.

I watched this nigga whisper in Melanie's ear, and when she giggled, I wanted to blow this entire bitch up.

My steps continued, and my pace quickened. I was unable to take any more of what I was watching. An abrupt end was about to come to the entire night.

After ordering Sinaa and Melanie to come on, I had to walk away before I put that nigga, who was still trying to spit game, down.

This was exactly why I stayed away from dealing with women outside of my normal parameters. Too much emotion had men thinking about risking their freedom for women. Nah, I needed my control, and my rules.

I finally looked back once I reached the entrance of the club to ensure Sinaa and Melanie were behind me.

Sinaa was close on my heels, but Melanie was a little further back, which told me she decided to continue a conversation with that lame after I walked away.

My gaze returned to Sinaa, and she had a confused look on her face. We've had several interactions with one another since she moved to Miami, but I'm sure she was still baffled by my current demeanor.

I was just glad she didn't ask for an explanation because I really didn't have one.

Melanie finally caught up to us, and I led the way to a waiting, blacked-out, chauffeured SUV.

Sinaa finally spoke.

"Is everything good, Warrick? Did Malachi tell you to come and check up on us?"

I rubbed my bearded chin, trying to figure out how to answer that. But before I could, Melanie interjected.

"Nah, Si. I think someone was jealous," she said and winked at me.

Sinaa whipped around to me, and a knowing smirk graced her lips.

"Ohhhh," she quipped, then broke out into a full grin.

She leaned over and whispered something into Melanie's ear,

but I couldn't make out what she was saying.

Melanie laughed like it was the funniest shit she ever heard.

When the car pulled up to Sinaa's house, I got out and opened the door for the ladies.

Sinaa thanked me for making sure they got home safe and sound before walking away.

Melanie tried to walk away without saying anything, but I pulled her ass back. She looked up at me with confusion laced in her big brown irises.

"Melanie, you are mine," I told her.

Her eyebrows drew together.

"Excuse me? I am no object, and I belong to no one. My recent divorce decree proves that. So, I'm not quite sure why you think otherwise. Especially since I don't know you and you damn sure don't know my ass."

That mouth.

I wanted to do several things to it, including pushing her to her knees and shove my dick down her throat.

"I promise you will see what I mean. In the meantime, keep these lames out of your face."

Melanie rolled her eyes and sucked her teeth.

"Goodnight, Warrick. I suggest you go home and clear the fog from your head, because you have me fucked up, sir."

My dick jerked in my pants. She had no idea what that last word falling from her lips did to me.

"We'll see. Goodnight, Melanie."

I conceded this round because I knew she wasn't ready for me. And I damn sure didn't know what control she was having over my body and mind... further proving that I was not ready for her ass either.

Melanie smirked.

"That's what I thought," she retorted before retreating into the house.

I watched her the entire way, enjoying the sway of her sexy hips, and big bubble butt.

Damn, that woman is gorgeous.

Chapter Eleven

MELANIE

"Mel, what the hell was that about?" Sinaa asked, wasting no time jumping on me when I crossed the threshold.

"What was *what* about?" Malachi's voice boomed as he turned into the large entryway.

I gave Sinaa a look which relayed, *you better keep ya damn mouth shut.*

"Nothing, baby. What are you doing up?" Sinaa asked, successfully changing the subject.

"You thought I was going to close my eyes knowing my wife and sister was out with niggas probably all in their face?"

"Baby, I only want you. Come," Sinaa grabbed my brother's hand, "Let me show you how much."

I wanted to gag in my damn throat. But I didn't want to draw any attention back to me. Plus, this was their house... they could do whatever nasty shit they wanted.

However, that only further fueled my ass to land one of these jobs and get my own place. Not that I couldn't already afford the condo I was interested in, being as though I had Gordon's money sitting pretty in my bank account. I just wanted to make sure I had a steady flow of income before I pulled the trigger on purchasing in Miami's high ass real estate market.

When I made my way up to my bedroom, so thankful that it was far away from Sinaa and Malachi's, I found myself lost in a sea of thoughts.

I was so confused by Warrick. He went from turning me down at my brother's wedding, to staking his claim over me.

That shit made absolutely no sense.

Tonight, was only the second time I've run into him since the wedding. And yeah, sparks flew each time, but I was so far out of my depth that I had no idea what any of those feelings actually meant.

But damn, if he ain't make my juices flow with excitement during every interaction.

I wanted to know more. I wanted to closely study the dominance that oozed from his being. I wanted him to devour me whole, leaving nothing in its wake.

Those thoughts alone scared the shit out of me. I wasn't sure any of those things were what I needed to feel so soon after getting a divorce from a man I shared most of my life with.

Nothing made any sense, and I believed the alcohol was fucking with my ability to string together coherent thoughts.

After a hot shower, I climbed in bed, naked and exhausted, trying to free myself from complicated thoughts.

Only, all that came were vivid fantasies of Warrick and his thick frame showing my body the pleasure it so desperately wanted. As my eyes felt weighted by the minute, my body relaxed, and gave way to blissful sleep–fueled with mouthwatering dreams of Warrick's deep chocolate skin and bulging biceps owning my body.

Chapter Twelve

MELANIE

"Naomi! Guess what?!" I rushed into the family room, ready to share my great news, or at least it was great news for me. It wouldn't be so great for Naomi or Zinae.

I'd only been in Miami for a few short weeks, and the stars were already aligning perfectly.

Naomi looked up from her laptop, and Zinae turned from the stove to see why I was so excited.

"What, Mama?"

"I got a job!"

"Congrats, Aunt Mel!" Zinae was the first to reply.

"That's great, mama!"

She was all smiles, and I felt glee before delivering my next words.

"It's at you girls' school! I'm the new African American Studies teacher," I boasted.

They both stopped what they were doing, and silence fell over the room.

"Zinae, don't burn your grilled cheese," I said with laughter filling my tone.

"You're kidding, right?" Naomi asked.

"Nope. I start next Monday."

She mumbled, "This is some bullshit."

"I heard that, little girl. Watch your damn mouth."

Sinaa burst through the doorway with her camera phone trained on the girls.

"Y'all want this footage for the YouTube channel, or naw?" She asked in a fit of giggles.

We were wrong, but it felt so damn good.

The girls both relaxed a little. I could already tell they were thinking they were being pranked by their moms.

"Oh, y'all got jokes," Zinae told Sinaa. "Good one."

I laughed harder.

"Dead ass," I confirmed. "Aren't you both glad you signed up for that class? I can't wait to be your teacher."

The disbelief returned to their features while Sinaa and I could not contain our mirth.

This was going to be fun as hell!

Zinae turned off the stove and abandoned her grilled cheese– I guess she wasn't hungry anymore.

Both girls then fled the open kitchen, family room combination, with attitudes clearly written on their faces.

"Is it bad that that felt so damn good?" Sinaa asked.

"Nope!" I popped my lips. "That's what their asses get."

We laughed harder, giggling like two schoolgirls over our victory.

"Maybe we should make our own YouTube channel and post this shit–tag them and everything.

"Sinaa, now *that* is wrong. But such a great idea."

Malachi walked into the kitchen and began questioning Sinaa and I immediately.

"What's so damn funny, and why the hell is my daughter and niece upstairs slamming shit around?"

I loved how serious Malachi took his fathering role. He never said *stepdaughter...* Zinae was his child, fully. And anyone could see the swoony-eyed look Sinaa got every time he spoke of Zinae.

"Mel just gave them the news that she'll be working at their school."

"Shit, y'all left me out of that conversation? That ain't right. I wanted to see that shit."

Malachi has been the subject of many viral videos, so I can only imagine the pleasure he would have taken in seeing their reaction.

"Don't worry, bro... we got it on film," I told him.

"That's what the fuck I'm talking about! Let's upload that shit and tag them."

"You and your wife are too much. She just said the same thing."

"We're within our rights. That damn video of me at the ice-skating rink is still getting hits. I deserve payback. I want justice."

Sinaa and I cackled.

Malachi was really in his feelings about that video. Whenever it popped up as a topic, he would catch a major attitude and be in his feelings.

"We gotta come up with a crafty YouTube name," I conceded.

Their energy was contagious, and they had me waiting in on their evil plan.

Malachi rubbed his hands together, and a sinister looked crossed his features.

"Bet."

I shook my damn head.

"Y'all think on it. I'm gonna go upstairs and change for the gym."

I had too much energy buzzing through my body. I needed a quick cardio session.

"Oh, and Malachi... I'm ready to pull the trigger on that condo. Draw up the paperwork if it's still available."

"No doubt, sis. I got you."

Chapter Thirteen

WARRICK

My usual routine was interrupted. I couldn't get Melanie off my mind, and nothing I did solved my damn issue.

I had no idea what her allure or appeal was, but she was all I wanted.

Weeks passed, and the only things that seemed to help was work because talking about sports always seemed to be my calming space—and the gym.

My body was sore as shit, but I was done tapping for the day.

Gym it is!

I could go to my other claiming place, but the club hadn't been doing anything for me lately. In fact, I was only able to go once since my last interaction with Melanie, and it was very uneventful.

Again, the gym it was.

I walked into the large workout space, and all I could do was let out a dry chuckle at how my thoughts led to the reminder of how small this damn city really was.

Fuck.

I continued my pace over to the weights, ignoring the sight of Melanie on the elliptical. Her ass was bouncing as she glided her legs.

I can't escape this damn woman.

I had to keep walking because I didn't want to disturb her and end up fucking her in the locker room of the damn gym.

Stacking the weights, I forced myself to focus on the energy I was getting ready to exert. I wanted nothing left vibrating through me when I completed my workout.

As I sat on the edge of the bench, my eyes connected with Melanie's in the mirror. She tried for nonchalance and continued with her workout.

I let my gaze fall and pushed through rep after rep. Of course, it was like magnetic energy. My eyes were automatically pulled in the direction of Melanie's.

She quirked a brow at me as she climbed off the elliptical and moved on to the next part of her workout.

When a dude entered her space and tried to give his assistance with one of the machines she was attempting to work, I put the weights I was supposed to be lifting, down.

My workout was done for.

I had no idea why my brain instantly went to blowing shit up when I saw another man in Melanie's space, but here I was again... thinking about how I wanted to rip that nigga's throat out and light his ass on fire afterwards.

I didn't even wipe away the sweat that was pouring off me. I strolled over to them, and stepped between Melanie and the lame, blocking his view of her.

"What did I tell you the last time we spoke, Melanie?" I

asked, glaring at her. Not even giving ole boy any of my attention, which he should've been thankful for.

Melanie bit her lip and gave me a look that told me I affected her, but she refused to answer my question.

The random dude interjected–I guess after recognizing me.

"My bad, War... I wouldn't even have looked her way... I didn't know that was you."

I turned to him, took him in, and gave a slight nod. Homie was smart enough to walk off after my nonverbal acknowledgment.

"So, are you gonna run every man off? But not even ask me on a date? That's pretty wack since you claim that I am yours. It seems to me that you don't even know how to treat me–again, someone you claim is yours. Why should I allow you to claim me?"

I stared back at Melanie and stroked my beard.

"Be ready tomorrow night... at seven."

Melanie rolled her eyes.

"Whatever, Warrick," she responded.

And my name on her lips made my dick come to life in my ball shorts.

I pulled Melanie to me. And I knew she felt the outline of my dick through the thin material we both had on.

"Careful. You're playing with fire, baby. Be ready."

I left her standing there, not allowing her a chance to use that smart ass mouth.

My patience with Melanie, and myself, was wearing me the hell down. And I couldn't word spar with her right now. Because I would end up balls deep in her pussy.

Chapter Fourteen

MELANIE

Warrick thought he would be picking me up and taking me on a date tonight. I, on the other hand, had a different set of plans.

I didn't need to be wooed; I needed to be fucked. It had been too damn long, and my body was craving strong hands. Warrick's hands, to be exact.

He kept telling me that I wasn't ready for him or to stop playing with fire, but Warrick was about to find out it was the other way around.

A firm knock on the door let me know he arrived, and I walked over to open it in all my naked glory.

When I swung the door open, Warrick's mouth dropped, but he collected himself almost instantly and smirked down at me.

"We're going to do things my way. I have had enough of you bossing me around," I told him. "You coming in?"

I didn't wait for his response. I knew his ass was coming in. So, I walked away, leaving the door wide open. I knew the sway of my bare hips would have him following.

As expected, Warrick followed after me, and I heard the locks click in place. It was as if the sound provided finality in what I knew was going to take place tonight.

Warrick's strides finally caught up to mine, and he gripped me by the waist, pulling me to him.

"This is how you want to do this?"

He squeezed my little love handles tighter, causing a burst of pleasurable pain to make its way through my body. The firmness of his grip had my honeypot dancing as if she knew she were about to be fed.

I bit my bottom lip and nodded my head up and down, melting into his chest.

"This is how I want to do this," I confirmed.

He walked us over to my island and bent me over.

I could not contain my excitement. He was about to get right to it, and I could not wait.

SMACK.

The loud sound reverberated through my apartment. And the sting of his hand making contact with my ass took me by total surprise.

Shit! I didn't know whether to be excited or scared.

My ass was stinging, but my pussy was also leaking juices down my inner thigh.

"Defiance won't get you what you want from me, Melanie."

SMACK.

Warrick's large hand connected with my other ass cheek, and my body jerked against the counter.

I was panting like crazy. Never have I ever had a man spank me. Ever.

It was something that I always balked at. But shit, the way I was about to orgasm when his palm connected with my ass... this is an avenue my ass should have been traveled.

Warrick massaged the sting out of each cheek, then spread my ass apart, exploring the slickness that was escaping my tight core.

"Ohhh, you're so wet. You like being spanked, huh?"

Warrick leaned over, whispering in my ear.

All I could do was moan.

Then his ass slipped one of his thick ass digits into my core, and my body liquified.

I was going to come, and hard.

"You better not fucking come. I didn't say you could. You come only when I give you permission to do so. And I'm still debating on whether I'm going to let you come tonight or not."

What the fuck?!

He better make me come or we're going to be fighting.

Warrick was already so in tune with my body, and he must've felt me stiffen at his words.

"Oh, you don't like that, do you? I told your ass you weren't ready for me."

He was moving his finger in and out of me at a devastatingly slow pace, and I wanted him to speed it up so bad.

"And here I was, trying to be a gentleman and take you out for a nice meal. But you wanted to tempt the savage in me. Well, baby... you have him."

His finger brushed against my swollen g-spot, but he immediately backed away, not giving me the pressure I needed.

"Please, I need to come, Warrick."

"I like to hear you beg, Melanie. But I'm still not going to give you what you want."

He pulled his finger from me and brought it to my lips, rubbing my juices over my plump bottom lip, then the top.

"Open," he commanded.

I guess I didn't react fast enough for him, because his other hand came down on my ass again, and the loud smack bounced off the walls.

The moan that escaped me caused my lips to part, and Warrick pushed his finger inside my mouth.

"Suck!"

His voice was so strangled. It was as if he were trying to keep control of whatever thoughts were circulating in his head. But I wanted him to come unglued.

I sucked hard on his finger, swirling my tongue around his thick digit. I wanted to give him a glimpse of what I was going to do to his dick when I got the chance. He needed to know what this mouth do.

"How do you taste, Melanie?"

I moaned.

SMACK.

"I asked, how do you taste?"

Oh, my goodness, I was about to come.

The entire scene was causing so much excitement, that I swear I was on the precipice just from the sound of his gravelly voice against my ear.

My body was shuddering at just the anticipation of release.

"You better not fucking come. You better hold that shit. You come and I will not touch you again."

A whimper escaped my lips.

The thoughts of not having his touch after getting just this small taste had my body inwardly weeping at the possible loss.

"I'm going to have to teach you a thing or two about me. First lesson, when I ask a question, I expect an answer. So, for the last time, how the fuck do you taste, Melanie?"

"Sweet, tangy... delicious."

My ass quickly responded because I did not want to lose his touch.

"Mm... I wonder if you taste as good as you smell."

Warrick spun me around, lifted me onto the countertop, and placed my hands on the edge.

"Do not let go of this counter. You understand?"

I nodded.

"I said, do you understand?"

"Yes," I let out breathily.

I have never been handled like this, and my brain could not gather the sense it needed to question what the hell I had gotten myself into. I believe my mind and body were in utter shock.

Warrick looked satisfied by my verbal response and spread my legs.

He leaned down and inhaled deeply once his face was level with the juncture of my thighs.

I watched his eyes close as if he were getting high off the scent of me.

It turned me the hell on, even more than I already was.

Warrick gripped my inner thighs and spread me apart even more. Then, his tongue was making contact with my womanhood.

We both let out a moan.

All I could do was feel and throw my head back.

Remembering his command about not coming, I prayed and hoped I could contain my release. Because I was so damn close.

The way Warrick's tongue circled my hole, with such precision... I was lost in a sea of feelings.

"Warrick," I moaned.

At the sound of his name on my lips, he sucked harder.

"Please, Warrick. I'm going to come."

"No."

That one simple word—command rather—put my ass right back in check.

However, as the minutes ticked by, my legs were beginning to shake as a result of almost reaching its limit.

Thankfully, Warrick must have known I couldn't take much more, and he stopped. I didn't want him to stop, but I also didn't want to come if that meant never feeling this again.

He made his way back up my body, kissing my bare skin as he rose.

When he reached my lips, he covered his mouth with mine and damn near kissed the life out of me, almost causing me to come... again.

God, I can't take no more.

"Please, Warrick," I begged for the umpteenth time, "I need to come. PLEASE!"

I was desperate, and I didn't even give a damn.

He pulled away from me and gazed deeply into my eyes.

"Tomorrow, be ready for dinner at eight. Defying me won't get you what you want, Melanie."

He kissed me one last time, leaving me on the counter, and headed for the door. As his hand reached out for the knob, he stopped and spun on his heels, looking me in the eye.

"And you better not touch yourself. That release is mine."

With that, Warrick was gone.

What the hell just happened?

I was stuck in total shock.

And my pussy throbbed, needing release.

I wanted to cry from sexual frustration. But I wouldn't touch myself. My ass was scared he would really be able to tell if I did.

Chapter Fifteen

MELANIE

. . . .

I was pissed. And horny.

Very fucking pissed and abso-fuckin-lutely horny.

Warrick stood me the hell up. My brain and pussy were seething.

What had my ass on ten, ready to pop up and fuck him up, was the fact that he had his got damn assistant call my phone to let me know he had some business meeting come up and that Warrick had to reschedule.

First of all, I never even gave that man my phone number.

I know his ass didn't get it from my brother. Because Malachi wanted me to become a nun after Gordon's ass. Have him tell it, all I need is him and the rest of the family—I don't need no man.

I had to point out to his ass that he couldn't be all the man I needed. Malachi gagged at that statement and left me the hell alone.

Knowing how Malachi felt, proved to me that Warrick

obtained my number from other sources. And I had no idea how. Shit, I was new to Miami and didn't know a damn soul.

Who cares how he got my number? But, to have my contact information, then have a fucking assistant call me. That shit rubbed me the wrong way and was bordering on disrespect.

Days passed, and I hadn't heard anything else from Warrick or his *assistant*.

To top that off, my silly ass was still holding out on pleasuring myself.

The lack of release was making this entire situation ten times worse than what it probably was.

Getting out of my car and strutting up to my brother's house, I entered and slammed the door behind me.

"Girl, what the hell is wrong with you? Slamming my shit like you pay bills in this muthafucka."

I rolled my eyes at Malachi. I really needed to talk to Sinaa, without my annoying baby brother snooping into our conversation.

"Where's Sinaa?"

"She's in her office. You good?"

Malachi turned serious for a second—I guess he was worried about my attitude being as though I rarely had emotional outbursts.

"I'm good, Khi. Just need to have some girl talk."

"Cool. Let me get out of y'all hair. I don't wanna hear whatever is bothering you, because I'm almost certain it has something to do with a man. As long as it ain't Gordon's ass, I'll chill... for the moment. I'll go get the girls from your place. The last thing I want is their asses to be sneaking around in an empty spot."

"You're gonna have to give them room to breathe at some point, Malachi."

"Yeah, when they're in college. And they are both going in-state, so I can still pop up on their asses."

I couldn't contain my laughter.

"Boy, bye!"

Malachi strolled away grumbling about they better not be with any peezy head lil' boys, and I laughed harder.

His antics were a nice distraction from my previous feelings of irritation.

But then, I headed to my sister-in-law's office, knowing that all those feelings were getting ready to come right back and smack me in the face.

Sinaa jumped up when I burst in the door of her office and damn near spilled the cup of tea she was holding.

"What the fuck, Melanie? What is wrong with you?"

"Why do you and your husband assume something is wrong with me?"

"Well, maybe because it seemed like you were the police busting in my damn door, ready to shoot first and ask questions later."

I plopped down on the chair opposite her desk and let out a loud groan.

"So, why did Warrick accost me at the gym, demand that I go out on a date with him, come to my house, but I was naked instead of dressed to go out. Then he spanks me, brings me to the edge of orgasm—multiple times, then leaves. Oh, and before he steps out of my door, he orders me to not make myself come. And now, he stood me up after ordering me to be ready for a real date the next night. He had his fucking assistant call and cancel on me."

"Ummmm... what?!" Sinaa's eyes were bugged out, and her mouth hung open. "When did you start seeing Warrick? Does Malachi know? I remember how weird he was acting that night we were out, but that seems like forever ago. Was that what that was about?"

Sinaa had diarrhea of the mouth, and looked confused as hell.

Shit, as far as I knew... we were both the hell confused.

"It's not really much to tell. Warrick and I have only been around one another a few times. But each time, the sparks between us were crazy explosive. Then the two times he's seen a man in my face, he ran them off or made me leave. Like that night at the lounge, and ended the encounter by telling me that I pretty much belong to him. And Malachi doesn't know shit! So, keep ya damn mouth shut."

Sinaa rolled her eyes and ignored my last comment.

"Wow, girl... that's some deep shit. I thought Malachi and I had love at first sight, but you and Warrick–I think you two have us beat. You've only seen the man a few times, he's already staked his claim over you, and he *spanked* you! How was that? The mental picture is steamy as hell. Almost makes me wanna ask Malachi to spank me."

"What did I just say?"

"What? He wouldn't know I got the idea from your little secret boo thang."

"Sinaa..." I said in a warning tone.

"Okay. Okay. Sorry. But really though... What the hell happens from here? I don't know much about Warrick, but from what I deduced from the few times I have interacted with him, while he hung out with Malachi, is that he's a very serious individual, who's about his shit. So, I doubt that he just forgot about you. He probably really did have a work engagement."

"Then why not call personally? Why the fuck did he think it was okay to have his assistant contacting me? I don't like that."

"I mean... you ain't never dealt with anyone on his level. We all know Gordon's ass was the bottom of the fucking barrel. So, maybe it was nothing to have his assistant making and changing his plans. I say don't overreact just yet."

"Ugh! You're right. Let me chill—just a little."

"That-a-girl! And when y'all do work this shit out, I want all the fucking details, because it sounds like he's into some dominance shit."

"Girl, whatever. I don't know about all that."

"If you say so, sis. I see it, so be careful. Maybe Malachi knows more about him. Maybe I can try to get details without telling him why."

"Sinaa, are you dumb?!" I shrieked. "First of all, you ask your husband about the personal details of another man, and he's gonna light this entire bitch on fire. Second, once you start down that road, you won't be able to keep your mouth shut, and my brother will know all my business. And I don't want or need that."

"Fine. But you have to promise to tell me more," Sinaa whined.

I looked at her and shook my damn head. She was over here acting like we were Naomi and Zinae, instead of two grown ass women. But she had become my closest friend since finding Malachi, so I guess I could share a little of the details.

"If there will be more to tell, because right now... I want to stick it to Warrick's ass and say *fuck him,* even if he does come back around."

"You know you're not going to do that. That man is sexy as

hell. Panty dropping fine. Dark chocolate skin, looking so smooth that you just wanna lick it up..."

I interrupted Sinaa's drooling ass.

"Um, did you forget that you're married to my brother?"

The dreamy-eyed look faded from her facial features, and Sinaa immediately looked sheepish.

"My bad. But shit... I can still appreciate a sexy Black man. My ass ain't blind."

"You're right. He is fine as hell, isn't he?"

"Too damn fine," Sinaa confirmed.

We went back and forth with jokes a little longer, and I had to admit that I felt much better.

I had no real answers with this situation regarding Warrick, but I knew that it wasn't like I was looking for my next husband, so I told myself to chill and see what comes.

And I really loved and appreciated Sinaa for making me see reason.

Chapter Sixteen

WARRICK

I don't know what the hell was wrong with me, but I knew having my assistant call and cancel on Melanie was a lame ass move. However, after getting a glimpse of her naked body, and a taste of her sweet center, Melanie had me a little shook.

Mainly because I was so close to losing control, tying her ass up, and taking her body.

She claimed that was what she wanted, but I still didn't believe she fully knew what she was getting herself into with me, and I was reluctant to tell her. Which has never been my style.

I was normally up front regarding my needs and wants. Not feeling any type of way about taking what I wanted then moving on.

But with Melanie, just a few short interactions had her embedded in my damn brain. Her taste was like a stain on my lips that I didn't want to get rid of. Her aura pulled me in.

She was consuming me, and I hadn't even had her yet. So, it was best for me to pause on our date.

Even though I had my assistant call Melanie, I still wanted her to know that she wasn't allowed to touch herself. So, I made sure my assistant relayed the message loud and clear.

Like I told her, I didn't make it a habit of repeating myself. Even if the commands weren't directly from my mouth. And while things were getting out of hand, fast... the morose part of me still wanted to own her first orgasm with me.

I'm sure Melanie was embarrassed by my assistant delivering the message, and that made me smirk.

A part of me also didn't want to call her directly, because I knew that mouth of hers would try and chew me the hell out.

While I didn't normally like disobedience, it lit a fire in me and turned me the hell on when Melanie did so. It was as if I wanted to own her mind, and body, but I also wanted her to continue to be the spitfire she was.

As much as her mouth was a turn-on, making Melanie wait was twofold. I needed to let her know that she did not control things. I also needed to make sure I had my own control and composure in check.

I really wanted her, and I knew I needed to slow walk her into what I expected from her. From the few encounters that we did have, she didn't seem to have a submissive bone in her body. And that... was what I needed.

But I still didn't want her to become meek. I knew my strategy would keep her on her toes and ready to go head-to-head with me.

The thought had my dick twitch. I was curious to see how much fight she had in her, and how far I would let her take it.

After the first week went by, I sent Melanie a nice bouquet of black-tie Camellias, with an assortment of red Rhododendrons. I attached a handwritten note to relay the new date and to be ready by seven that evening.

I chose the flower combination because I wanted them to match the beautiful energy and aura she exudes and express the passion she was pulling out of me.

But let's see how well you follow directions.

I would love nothing more than to punish Melanie if she disobeyed me this time around.

Needing to get my body under control and ready for our date later, in addition to attempting to get my mind right for whatever direction Melanie and her mouth went, I headed to the gym.

I could have just worked out at home, but for total separation from my thoughts, I needed to be away from my home and all the surfaces that I could likely bring pleasure–and pain–to Melanie.

As soon as I pulled into the lot of Onyx Fitness, a Black-owned gym, I regretted my decision to leave the house.

I saw Malachi walking out of the gym to his ride as I was approaching the door.

"What's going on, Warrick?"

I could already tell by the tone of his voice; he was about to be on some bullshit.

Malachi and I were good friends, due to me volunteering my free time to his team's coaching staff during the NFL off-season. I love supporting my Alma mater and tried whatever I could to stay out of trouble.

Naturally, I took to Malachi as he was talented, and I thought he had what it took to go pro. I was surprised when he decided to not push through what I considered a small injury and go into real estate. Nevertheless, I supported him in that also, and allowed him to find me my last two homes.

"What's going on, Malachi?"

"Nah, see. You my boy. And we cool as shit. You know I look up to you like an older brother, but I can't sit here and *keke* with you. My wife told me that you ran into her and my sister a while back, and you were extra flirtatious with Melanie. My wife then proceeded to tell me how she thought y'all would make a *cute couple.* You see my problem with that, right?"

I let out a breath, closed and opened my eyes.

This was a conversation I didn't want to have. This was also a part of my reason for delaying reaching back out to Melanie. I didn't want to mess up my relationship with Malachi.

But honestly, he would just have to deal, because Melanie was a grown ass woman.

"Yo Khi, I don't want to fight with you. You're like my little brother, and I want to keep the peace."

"Then, as my brother, you should have known that my sister was off-limits, Warrick. You know better. And if you didn't know better... why the hell would you think I would be okay with you getting my sister into the shit you're into?"

"First, Melanie is a grown ass woman... older than you. Second, you think you know about my life and the *shit I'm into,* but you don't know shit, Khi. I would never harm your sister in any way. I'm attracted to Melanie. And all I'm currently doing is taking her out on a date."

"You're taking her out on a date?!" He reared back in disgust."
Shit.

I assumed that because he knew about me running into Melanie and his wife, he knew the rest.

"Again, it's just a date, Malachi."

"I'on like that shit, Warrick."

"You don't have to like it. But you will respect your sister's choice."

Malachi looked at me greasy. I was keeping it real, though. If Melanie and I became involved, Malachi would mind his fucking business... by choice or by force.

We stood toe to toe, eye to eye, neither backing down from whatever we were feeling.

He didn't want to, but he finally stepped back, giving me one last evil glare.

"You hurt my sister, and I'm gonna fuck you up. Remember that."

I chuckled at that.

"Just mind your business, Malachi."

I walked right past his sour ass.

I really need that workout now.

———

I looked in the mirror, making sure I was satisfied with my appearance. I decided to keep it casual with a pair of slacks and a white shirt, leaving it unbuttoned at the neck.

Leaving the house, I was wondering what I would find when I arrived at Melanie's. If she wasn't dressed to go out, I wasn't sure what I would do.

She was testing and poking the bear, and she didn't even know it.

I'm sure she knows a little by now after our previous interaction, but that was just the tip of the iceberg.

Knocking on the door, I held my breath.

I hadn't been this excited about taking a woman out in a good while. Hell, I haven't taken a woman out in forever. I normally would find women who I knew could handle my lifestyle through a *dating service*. Or an exclusive club I frequented.

But getting one glance at Melanie, all that shit seemed to be an afterthought and really unappealing.

A grin spread across my face as Melanie came into full view upon opening her door wide.

She donned a floral jumpsuit that stopped and cropped around her calves. On her feet, Melanie had on a pair of high, simple strap, nude heels.

I was pleased that she was actually ready for a night out.

"You look beautiful, as always," I told her.

Melanie smiled up at me. Even with her tall stilettos, she barely reached my chin. I wanted to bring her to me and taste her lips, but I maintained my control by not touching her just yet.

I knew the minute I allowed myself to bask in the feel of Melanie's soft skin, there was no coming back.

"You're not looking too bad yourself, Warrick. Where are we headed?"

"A jazz club. Come."

I took Melanie by the hand and led her to the elevators and down to the lobby of her condominium.

Of course, Malachi would have it no other way than his sister residing in one of the best condo buildings in Miami. And even though we were going to have issues in the near future, I was glad Malachi took proper care of his sister. That, I could appreciate one hundred percent.

But the thought of taking over that care quickly crossed my mind.

Once outside, Melanie was surprised when I deactivated the alarm to my G-Wagen.

"I took you for a more of a fancy sports car kind of guy."

"Nah, I'm entirely too big for that shit. I own one, but I don't ever drive it."

I opened the door for her and bent to strap her seat belt. I really just wanted to be near her and smell her fragrant scent, so I allowed myself this pleasure.

Melanie smirked at me as if she knew I wanted to do more than strap her into her seat.

You have no idea what I really want to strap you to.

My thoughts went straight to my dick, and I fought control to keep my throbbing manhood in check. But the image of Melanie being strapped to my bed, to the chair, my Saint Andrew's Cross... really the thought of her being bound period was almost too much for my control.

She's not ready for that, War.

Shit. My self-control was really being tested. And I wasn't exactly sure why I was even going to these lengths to hold it off.

I did know that a huge part of me wanted Melanie, and there was a slight fear that she wouldn't accept me and all my... acquired tastes.

So, for that reason alone, I was going to try and be as normal as possible.

Melanie seemed like the girl that wanted normal.

And for some unfathomable reason, I wanted to try... for her.

Chapter Seventeen

MELANIE

This was nice.

Warrick escorted me inside of a beautiful jazz club that was decorated to appear as if it were straight out of the Harlem Renaissance. And being as though I was from New York, I fell in love with it instantly.

The staff was dressed to the nines, fulfilling that dreaminess of that era.

The performers were crooning all the Black greats. It was an entire vibe, and I was glad my ass decided to listen to orders and be ready on time. I wouldn't have wanted to miss this for anything.

My mom loved music from that era. Listening to the singer perform a Billie Holiday song brought back such fond memories of my parents. They were young, but they had old souls, which I contributed to being born and raised in such a historical city.

Warrick leaned over and whispered in my ear.

"Are you okay? Do you not like jazz?"

I leaned back into him and inhaled his manly scent.

"I'm fine. This just makes me think of New York, where I'm from, and of my parents. They loved this music."

He smiled down at me. And my god!

The way his straight, white teeth shined through his dark, thick beard... my kitty cat was jumping. Then remembering the little sample of tongue he gave me the last time we were together, she was down there dancing around as if she were chasing a ball of yarn waiting for her prize.

Whew—my thoughts were all over the damn place.

"I'm glad you like it. Malachi told me your parents passed years ago. I'm truly sorry for your loss."

It was my turn to smile up at him.

"Thank you. I appreciate that. It's hard, but I'm glad for all of the lessons they taught us when they were alive."

Warrick nodded at me, and we fell into a comfortable silence, enjoying our surroundings.

The food and drinks we ordered were delicious and they fit so well with the theme of the spot. I didn't want the night to end unless Warrick granted me permission to come. Then... my ass was ready to leave now!

"Penny for your thoughts," Warrick asked, smirking at me.

I chuckled because his ass knew the direction of my thoughts.

And I didn't want to pussyfoot around anything. My ass was desperate for release.

"If you'll grant me release... sir."

I added *sir* because I pretty much gathered the type of shit he was into and did a little research. I had no personal experience dealing with Doms, and I was sure I was not meant to be a submissive, but I would play along—a little.

Warrick cocked his head to the side and stared at me with curious orbs.

"*Sir,* huh?"

I shrugged.

"After the other night, I thought you'd like that title."

He barked out a laugh in response.

Okay, maybe he doesn't like it.

I was confused.

I had no idea what the hell I was doing. I hadn't been on a date in over fifteen damn years. And never have I ever come across a man like Warrick.

"And why did you think I would like that title?"

I shrugged again.

"I dunno. I did a little research after you left; you throwing out commands and shit had me curious."

"And what did your research reveal?"

"That you were likely a Dom."

"And what did you learn about Doms?" His questions continued.

"That they like control and like submissive partners."

"And are you a submissive, Melanie?"

"To be honest, no–I don't think so."

"Yet you decided to go out with me. Why?"

"If I'm honest, there seems to be this pull between us. I've never felt anything like it. Not even with my husband of fifteen years."

Warrick nodded but didn't reply. He looked to be deep in thought.

The silence carried for so long that it was making me anxious and unable to stay still in my seat.

I decided to break the silence since it didn't seem like he wanted to continue the conversation.

"Will you allow me to come tonight?" I asked, on pins and needles, awaiting his response.

He blessed me with his sexy smile and pushed back from the table.

"Let's dance."

What the fuck?

This man had me thrown all the way off, and I didn't know how to right myself or my thoughts. It was frustrating–and exciting.

I didn't know what to say.

So, I got my butt up from the chair, rested my hand in Warrick's large one, and allowed him to lead the way to the center of the dance floor.

It was as if a path was cleared for his large stature, as he owned his strides with perfection.

In the thick of the dance floor, I felt a little shy. There weren't many other couples dancing about. And Warrick stood out among the partygoers, in turn, making me stand out.

However, as soon as he pulled my smaller frame against his large, solid body, everything around us faded to black. Warrick's hands felt like magic on my body. And that magic wiped away all the shyness and negative thoughts that swirled around in my mind.

It was as if his presence alone commanded my body to calm, which she happily obliged.

Warrick's gipped was so tight and possessive. It turned me the hell on, and I felt the ever tell of slickness began to pull in the seat of my panties.

Leaning down and whispering in my ear, Warrick said, "You want release, Melanie?"

I could barely control my breathing.

This man had me short-circuiting.

"Yes, please," I managed a breathy reply.

And right there on the dance floor, Warrick brought his lips down to mine in a heated, passionate kiss as he continued to rhythmically sway to the beat.

The feel of his thick, full lips, and the scratchiness of his beard, had me moaning into his mouth.

My moan allowed Warrick to slip his tongue in my mouth, and he stroked it along my own, mimicking the cadence of the music.

He was controlling my tongue just as he did my clit weeks ago, and I was losing my damn mind.

I swear I didn't know it was possible to orgasm from a simple kiss – well, there wasn't anything simple about this kiss – but still... I didn't know the tingling in the pit of my belly could be awakened with the connection of lips alone.

Nevertheless, here I stood, with my body having a mind of its own, as body shivers moved through me, and moans of ecstasy fell from my lips.

Warrick swallowed my moans as he continued our kiss. He had me unhinged, and coming, right there in the middle of the dance floor.

From a kiss?

My brain was complete mush, but I was still astonished at my body's reaction.

Warrick backed away from our kiss, but continued to hold me tight to his chest as tremors continued to take over my muscles.

"Was that the release you were looking for?" He asked.

I melded into his chest further, leaving no room for anything to come between us, not that I would let it anyhow.

Cause... shit... I wish a muthafucka would.

Pump ya brakes, Mel.

I was standing here getting all possessive and whatnot. That was so unlike me. I didn't even care to stake claim to Gordon, and that man was my husband.

"That was... I have no words." I finally responded after gathering my thoughts.

Warrick's soft chuckle invaded my ears, and his dick jerked against my stomach. I could feel the girth of it right through his slacks.

Well... shit!

"Can we get out of here, and can I have more?" I boldly asked.

"What? You think I'm the type of guy to put out on the first date?"

I pulled back from his hold, and strained my neck to look up at him.

He's serious!

Before I could even spew together a response, Warrick playfully tapped me on the tip of my nose and answered my question.

"Not tonight, Mel."

I smiled wide. He had never called me *Mel,* and I had to admit that I liked the intimacy of him using my nickname. But I was also disappointed by his response. I didn't push, though. Something told me that he would enjoy punishing me, and if that came in the form of making me wait longer, I'd die.

I nodded my head in understanding and continued to let him guide my body to the beat of the music.

It had been less than a year since my divorce, and I couldn't really conclude why I was giving so much energy into a man I barely knew.

A small part of me was wondering if I was simply rebounding, but there was the *thing* about Warrick. I couldn't put my hand on it, but my body wanted parts.

————

Once our night was over – a night I would never forget, Warrick drove me back home, walked me up to my door, and kissed me so good, I almost came again.

God, I need to feel his dick.

I guess I shouldn't be asking God for a sinning action, but dammit... Warrick was making me desperate.

"Night, Mel. I'll have to come scoop you so we can do this again."

"You sure you don't want to come in?" I damn near whined like a toddler.

Warrick laughed at my desperation, and I didn't even care. I just wanted him to bring my body pleasure, because everything about his touch told me I would be in for an experience I've never had.

"Go inside, Melanie," Warrick ordered.

I sighed and slid through the door to my condo.

Once I was on the other side, I leaned my head against the solid wood, and let out a deep breath.

"Well, he didn't say I couldn't touch myself," I said out loud.

"Fucking nasty, Mel!"

I damn near jumped out of my gad-damn skin at the sound of my brother's voice.

I whirled around and found Malachi lounging in the chaise by my little reading nook, off to the left of my living room.

"Malachi Long! What the fuck are you doing in my condo?!"

"I came here to warn you about Warrick, but from the sound of things, it seems like I'm too late. So, I'll say this... I don't like that shit, Mel."

"You need to mind your fucking business. I am a grown ass woman and can make my own damn decisions. Or did you forget that I am five years older, took care of your ass, and figured out a way for you to get everything *you* wanted in life? I have never experienced happiness, and I'm not blaming you for that, but if I'm currently happy at the moment—whether it's fleeting or not—can you just back off."

I think my sexual frustration was fueling my attack on my brother, but I was the hell grown. And not to mention I forgone my fun phase in life to appear as the responsible adult to my young and impressionable brother.

But that was probably only two percent of my current feeling.

What I really wanted was some dick.

My nosy ass brother just happened to be the first one in my line of aggregated fire.

"Damn, Mel. Calm down. I'm just looking out for you. You don't know all of what Warrick is into. That shit ain't for the weak."

My eyes damn near bugged out of my head.

"Are you calling me weak, Malachi?!" I yelled across the room.

Thankfully he had enough sense to not be within arm's reach

of me, because I would've knocked his big ass head off his shoulders.

Ugh! What does Sinaa see in his annoying ass?

"You know that's not what I meant."

"Do I?"

"Man, Mel... that nigga be having women chained and be beating them and shit."

I shrugged.

"Maybe I'll like it."

"You know what," he said and stormed past me to my door.

Good. Get out.

"Don't call me when Warrick breaks your heart because you can't handle what he's into."

"Get the fuck out, Khi. NOW!"

Tears were threatening behind my eyelids. Malachi's words got to me. But I'd be damned if I would show my hand and prove his point. So, I held it together long enough for him to stomp out of my condo, slamming my door.

I walked into my room, disrobing along the way. I didn't give no fucks about Warrick and his rules.

We're not even together, I told myself.

Because I *was* going to have a round with my Rose in the shower. I may even follow that up with my big chocolate vibrating dildo once I climbed into bed.

Chapter Eighteen

MELANIE

Sinaa stood at my door with a large Frappuccino from what has become my favorite spot, Grovin' Bean Coffee Bar and Lounge.

I rolled my eyes, but snatched the drink out of her hand and walked back inside, leaving the door open.

"I'm sorry for Malachi, Mel."

I whirled around at her.

"You knew he was coming here to be a pain in my ass and didn't warn me?"

"Absolutely not. He came home on fire last night, and finally, after a lot of coaxing..."

I groaned, cutting her off, because I didn't want to hear that shit.

"Chill. I wasn't going to say anything inappropriate. So, like I was saying... he finally told me what went down between you two. He's sorry. I can assure you Malachi is going to show up here, or pop up on you wherever and apologize. I thought I'd at least soften you up, so you won't kill my husband."

I groaned again. But my annoyance was fading.

Sinaa was so damn adorable with her little pixie cut and freckles, damn near begging me not to strangle her man.

"The girls are good?" I asked, changing the subject.

"Yup, been up all night doing what they normally do... putting on for their YouTube followers."

We both laughed at that.

If there was anything that could melt my icy demeanor, it was my daughter and niece. They were going into beautiful, smart young women, and they made Sinaa, Malachi and I proud.

"You dropping them off at school tomorrow, or you want me to come get them tonight?"

They might as well live together because they barely spend the night away from one another. I'm so glad I got a three-bedroom condo instead of the two-bedroom condo.

"No, you can leave them where they are. I take care of them in the morning."

"Thanks, Si."

She waved me off, and got comfortable on the sofa, tucking her feet under her.

"So, what happened? Malachi told me you went on a date with Warrick. He also told me how he ran into him before your date and threatened him."

I rolled my eyes heavenward.

"He gets on my last nerve," I said.

Sinaa laughed.

"Well, look here... I love my man, and I have no doubt he can hold his own. But you keep your man in check. Warrick is huge, and I don't want him getting into it with Malachi. You tell his ass that I spent the last almost two decades in Tennessee, and we love our guns. I might not be able to beat his ass, but I will pull out my shotgun if I need to."

I cannot contain my laughter. The image of Sinaa's tiny frame wielding a shogun tickled me to my soul.

"Girl, it will not come to all of that. I told Malachi to chill the fuck out. And he better heed my warning or else he'll have to deal with me. He doesn't want that."

Sinaa nodded in agreement.

"You're probably right. I think my husband is a little scared of his big bad sister. Especially after watching you hold a knife to Gordon's dick."

We continued to go back and forth with our jokes, and we cannot control our mirth.

God, I needed this distraction.

I love that I now have Sinaa in my life. I never had too many friends. Because duh—Clarington was too damn small to get close to anyone. I refused to have my business out in the damn street.

And somehow, everyone still knew all my dirt.

After Sinaa left, I pretty much lounged around all day, enjoying the peace and quiet. I know eventually the girls will come back here to terrorize me when they tire of Malachi, so I had to bask in walking around naked while I could.

Finally, I decided to act like I had some sense and went over some grades and lesson plans for the week. I liked to keep it fresh, and so far, the kids in my class were enjoying having a new, younger teacher.

I was so deep in thought, that I damn near jumped out of my skin when my phone rang.

I didn't recognize the number, but it was a 305-area code, so that told me it was someone here in Miami.

"Hello," I answered cautiously, having no idea who was on the other end of the line.

"Good evening, Melanie. Are you enjoying your Sunday?"

Mmm... that deep baritone could not be mistaken.

"Warrick. Hello. I am enjoying my Sunday. How did you get my number?"

Come to think of it, how did this man get my address?

I didn't give him any information on me. And I know damn well Malachi didn't give it to him.

He's rich... I'm sure he has his ways, I told myself.

I probably should have been alarmed, but I wasn't. I was feeling good at the idea of him going through whatever lengths to maintain a connection to me.

"I have my ways," he responded.

Like I knew he would, he didn't give me any intel.

"Careful, Mr. Jones... people don't take well to stalking."

"You're not people, Melanie. You're mine."

"There you go again with that word. If I were yours, you shouldn't have left me needy last night, having to satisfy and release my own sexual tension."

Warrick focused on the fact that I pleasured myself, nothing else.

"Did I say you could touch yourself?"

"First, you can't tell me what I can and can't do to *my* body. Second, you didn't say I couldn't touch myself."

I smirked into the phone, wishing I could see his face.

"That mouth... it's going to get you in trouble."

"*Ohhh... I've been a bad girl. Punish me please,*" I mocked.

I didn't get the reaction I was looking for. The other end of the line was completely silent.

"Warrick, you there?"

"I'm here. Just contemplating your punishment."

The grit in his voice had me squirming in my seat. My pussy was exalting at the timber of his voice, and my mouth was panting from want and need.

"I can hear your hitched breathing on the line, so I know you didn't hang up. Does it turn you on... thinking of me punishing you, Melanie?"

I was a boneless mess of just... goo. My body slumped further into my chair, and my clit throbbed.

Because, *hell yeah...* I was turned on by the thoughts of a painful, yet pleasurable punishment, if it was being doled out by Warrick. However, I still didn't know what to think of my excitement about the idea. I had never thought of exploring this road of sexual activity, and I was really confused. I felt like it should be bad for some reason. But the way my clit couldn't stop jumping, it felt oh so right.

Finally, a little ashamed, I whispered into the phone.

"Yes."

I said it so low, because for whatever reason, I felt like I didn't want God to hear my response.

Warrick must've known that I was embarrassed, and he decided to flex on me.

"I can't hear you, Melanie. I'm going to need you to speak up, baby."

And there went another clit flip... the way, *baby,* sounds rolling off his lips... my ass was ready to invite him over.

"Warrick... I... this is different from anything I've ever felt."

"And that's okay, baby. All I need to hear is that you want to test things out with me, in bed. Because, Melanie, I will not lie to you. I don't have more to offer at the moment."

His words were like ice cold water being thrown right on my snatch.

Not that I wanted more from him than a mind-blowing fuck, but it angered me that he staked his claim so hard over me, yet all he has for me is a big dick and a few spankings.

Fuck that shit!

"I'll pass. Thanks, though."

I heard Warrick shift in his chair on the other side of the line. I'm sure my words took him by surprise.

"Did I say something wrong?" He asked.

It was a genuine question, and I swear... men were so damn dumb sometimes.

But I didn't have time to play games. I did that shit for far too long with a man who was an utter waste of my energy. I wasn't about to give anyone else the power to drain me.

And so far, things with Warrick have been confusing, bordering on draining, because I was so damn horny.

"Look, Warrick. I'm not sure what games you are playing, but I'm over it. I never asked you for anything. And I definitely never asked you for more of... well... nothing. Because that is what we are to one another. Nothing. I just ended a long, drawn-out marriage. I don't want anything from you. Well, maybe a few orgasms. Nevertheless, I never asked you for more. You are the one who staked some weird ass claim over me. And while I was intrigued by your fascination with me... *more* never crossed my mind."

More silence.

I was over it.

"You know what? Call me when the cat no longer has your tongue. But in the meantime, know you do not own me or my orgasms. They are mine... to give to whomever the fuck I want. Goodbye, Warrick."

I hung up on his ass.

Because shit. He had me fucked up.

Chapter Nineteen

WARRICK

Well, I fucked that up.

I sat at my desk confused as hell by the conversation that Melanie and I just had. It was going in the right direction, but my ass had to go and explain that I couldn't provide more.

I just felt like I needed to make my intentions known. Leaving room for confusion was never my thing. And normally, women were grateful for it. However, apparently, I was dealing with a different type of woman.

And she was right. She never asked me for more.

It was me who felt the need to claim her. It was my own body that would betray me and have me in my feelings when I saw her. I wanted to claim her. Own her. Provide her with pleasure I'm sure her body has never known.

But what I wasn't ready for were the possessive feelings I felt when she was with other men.

That shit didn't normally bother me.

I was a Dominate, yes. But I never wanted more than a few scenes with women. I have never wanted to actually collar any of the Submissives.

With Melanie, the thought of getting her a custom collar had my dick swelling to the point of pain.

The image of her kneeling before me, with my collar clasped tight around her neck.

Shit!

I was losing my fucking mind.

As much as I liked to play, I have never even considered collaring a woman. I wanted shit done my way, while in the moment, and I wanted to go on about my fucking day.

But with Melanie... the urge to make her mine was strong. And annoying, because I barely knew the damn girl.

I was never one to believe in the universe, divine intervention, and destiny... shit like that... I was the master of my own damn universe. However, it seems as though I was getting a crash course in some kismet shit I didn't even believe in.

I grunted and adjusted my dick, because my dude was still zeroed in on the image of Melanie on her knees and collared.

These were one of the times I wish I had a homie to talk to. But most people only assumed shit about my lifestyle. No one really knew.

The closest person to me who knew about my particular tastes was Malachi. And that's only because, for a short while, when I thought he was bound for the NFL, I took him under my wing... and introduced him to the lifestyle at one of my clubs.

But there was no way I could talk to him about this shit.

I saw the look in his eyes that day at the gym.

He already wanted to kill a muthafucka.

Welp, I didn't have anyone to talk to, so I guess I would settle for my usual therapy.

The gym it was.

I'd deal with my feelings, and Melanie, later.

Chapter Twenty

MELANIE

Mondays always come way too fast, but with my new teaching position, I loved Mondays. The sound of that first bell always had me excited to spread the knowledge of strong Black people in history.

Also, Naomi and Zinae were in my class. Because African American Studies was an elective, all grades could sign up for the class. And of course, ninety-eight percent of my students were Black. I wished more White people felt the need to know the history of the people their ancestors oppressed, but ignoring issues regarding Black was this country's response to everything.

But let it be a damn endangered animal, or an abused dog... they're storming the Senate, demanding policy change.

I had to shake my head at my damn self. My mind always went on a random tangent when I thought about my class makeup.

Students began to fill my class and take their seats. I kept an eye on the clock, because Naomi and Zinae thought that I wouldn't dig into their ass at school about arriving late to my class, especially when I knew their behinds arrived at school on time.

They both strolled in with about ten seconds to spare.

I swear they were testing me.

I cut my eyes at them, but started class without any interruptions.

"Happy Monday! I hope you all had a great weekend and are ready to continue to learn about the amazing Black trailblazers in our history."

A chorus of, *Good Morning, Ms. Long,* was yelled out. Some enthusiastically, some not so much.

I'm sure it was my annoying ass girls who sounded lackluster.

"This week, we are focusing on the amazing Black women in history. Black women have always been instrumental to the growth and development, not only to the Black community, but also to the world in general.

Right here in America, we had Black women who nursed White babies, birthed abolitionists and were abolitionists. There were Black women who refused to give their seats up because of their skin color, little Black girls braving all white schools, and Black women fighting for their rights to votes... I could go on and on. There are so many monumental Black women within the Black culture.

But let's dive deeper. Let's go back to the land of Africa. Let's study what these amazing women did before they were even stolen and forced on this foreign land."

Some of the students were nodding, excited to learn, as I was to teach.

That was the one great thing about this class being an elective. Most of my students wanted to be here. It was amazing to see the youth wanting to be connected to their history. In today's climate, I think all these kids needed to know where they have been so they can decide where they are going and the best path to take to get there.

It was just so rejuvenating to see.

"So, with that introduction, I start y'all off with an easy question. Can anyone tell me the name of the group of all-women warriors that the Dora Milaje are based on?" I crossed my arms, right over left, over my chest. "Y'all do know who they are, right?"

I got a few giggles with that. Then a chorus of *yeses.*

But all their asses were silent on providing the name of the all-female military.

"Nobody?"

Zinae raised her hand.

I knew she would know. She was one of my brightest students. Being homeschooled most of her life had her ahead of damn near every student in the school. She could've skipped to her senior year, but she wanted to stay with Naomi longer, so she declined. However, she still took every college course available to high schoolers. Not to mention that she was a helluva dancer and has been hired several times by Disney and teen girl groups to choreograph dance routines.

My niece was going places.

And I hope she took her damn sister right along with her, because Naomi was not as interested in school. But I had hopes for my little girl. She still had time to get it together.

"Yes, my beautiful niece?"

I knew I shouldn't put them on blast like that, but it was get back time, and I was going to enjoy my moment.

Speaking of which, Malachi, Sinaa, and I still have to upload our video.

Zinae groaned.

"*Ms. Long,*" she stressed my name as if to warn me to address her as if she was just another student. But the class already knew, so I didn't give a damn. "The answer is, The Dahomey Warriors. Also known as Ahosi—king's wives, and Mino—our mothers."

"Great, Zinae."

I turned my attention back to the class.

"These powerful Black women protected their king and their Kingdom of Dahomey, which is now known as Benin."

I went over some additional facts, and before I ended the class, I assigned everyone to come to my next class prepared to present at least two facts.

Again, most of the class genuinely looked excited. The joy that brought me made me a little sad that I decided to stay out of the workforce for so long.

Another thing I would never get back from my trifling ass ex-husband.

When class dismissed, I sat back in my chair until I heard yelling out in the hall.

I groaned.

This was the part of teaching that I absolutely did not like. Teenagers and their damn hormones could be draining some days.

I jumped up even faster and put a little pep in my step when I heard Naomi's voice calling someone a *bitch*.

When I got into the hall, Zinae was holding Naomi back, telling her to calm down.

"What is the problem?!" I asked.

The girl, I'm assuming Naomi had words with yelled out into the crowd.

"Aww... get mommy to come and save you."

I wanted to pluck that little girl from the damn and smack her teeth out. But I remained the ever-professional teacher.

"Young lady, I suggest you choose your tone and your words wisely."

She sucked her teeth. And again, I wanted to smack them from her mouth.

"All three of you, in my office. Now!"

I pointed to the door, and I gave a look to all three girls, wishing that any of them would even consider disobeying me.

Wisely, they all moved their ass.

"Now what is going on?" I asked, slamming my door.

"She started it," Naomi said, pointing at the other girl.

I rolled my eyes. Naomi sounded like a five-year-old.

I turned to the other girl. "What's your name?"

"Aja," she said and rolled her eyes.

Ohhh... this lil' heffa!

She was working my damn nerves.

"Well, Aja, you want to tell me what's going on?"

"No, not really. You can ask your daughters, or your nieces, whatever incestuous shit y'all got going on. Like, how is she your daughter, and that one your niece, but they are sisters? Shit is fucking disgusting."

I saw Naomi attempting to get back up out of her seat.

I cut my eye at her. "Sit down," I gritted out.

"But, mama! That's why I cursed her out."

"I said sit down, Naomi. And be quiet."

The only one looking unbothered by all of this was Zinae. No doubt she wanted to ignore whatever was being said, but I knew my baby girl wasn't built that way. She was built to buck, and I don't even know how the little New Yorker came out of her when her ass ain't even been there. I guess it's genetic.

I was angry too, and I knew I couldn't handle this situation by myself, because I didn't want there to be any issues of bias. So, I called the assistant principal down to my room.

I was glad that I had a free block. Because trying to deal with this and a class that was in session... was not the move.

And just when I thought I loved Mondays, and my job.

Ughh.

Once we were all settled, the problem became clear.

Aja was among the top ranking in the school, and she felt threatened by Zinae. Zinae, who could care less, ignored Aja's jab, but Naomi felt the need to defend her big sister. But Aja took her little jokes too far, and especially in front of me.

But to remain neutral, both Naomi and Aja got detention. And Zinae was free to go about her business.

"Here's a late slip. Get to your next class," I told all three girls, but not before I gave Naomi a look that told her I was going to talk to her ass this evening.

I didn't like drama. And I get the reason behind her snapping, but she had to learn not to be so damn quick with the lip. Especially when the hate is so clearly visible. I need to make sure to tell her to let them haters hate and for her to continue to do her, shine, and keep them mad, while she does nothing but prosper.

Once my room was cleared out, I enjoyed the next thirty minutes of peace, before preparing for my next class.

Dammit, Monday! Why did you have to go and fuck up my mood.

Chapter Twenty-One

WARRICK

I must have really pissed Melanie off because she was not answering my calls.

Damn. What did I do? I asked myself.

Two weeks without talking to her and not being in the mood for my normal club scenes had a brotha damn near suffering from blue balls.

And I was ready to put an end to that shit.

I was still confused as to what degree, but I wanted Melanie, and no amount of coaxing was allowing my body to say otherwise.

So, I guess my ass was going to do a pop up on her. I knew that was risky, but if she really wanted me to bounce out of her space, I would. And I would command my dick to get over her. Especially being as though we haven't even felt her walls wrapped around us.

My decision was made. I hopped in my truck and headed to her condo.

Parking in the garage—which a normal person off the street wouldn't be able to do, being as though Melanie lived in a secured condo—I made my way to the elevators, enjoying the luxuries of knowing people.

My name also garnered me access past the security desk with clear access to Melanie's front door.

I had to admit that I was a little nervous about this pop-up. Melanie seemed to be a loose cannon, and I wasn't sure how I would be received.

All of this was out of my norm. And I still wasn't sure what the hell I was doing—in the moment—or with Melanie in general.

However, I wasn't turning back now.

I was going to take Melanie's words for face value.

She said she wasn't looking for anything serious, and she cursed my ass out with that mouth that I've grown to like so much with assuming she did.

Giving those disclaimers was simply how I normally operated, I didn't think Melanie would take it the way she did.

After knocking twice, I stood turned away from the door a little, with my hands stuffed in the pockets of my slacks.

"Coming," I heard Melanie yell on the other side of the door, and my dick hardened at the sweet sound of her angelic voice.

I hadn't had sex in what felt like forever—another unusual thing for me, and I was ready to be buried inside of Melanie. I wanted to hear her screaming that exact word while I brought her to pleasure heights she's never known.

And I know she never has, because she came too fast with just the right touch to her sweet pussy lips.

She has no idea what else I could do to her body, I thought. But I was determined to show her.

The door swung open, and Melanie greeted me in a long sheer robe with a black tank and lace panties underneath.

Got Damn! She's fine as fuck!

No wonder my ass has been stuck on her. She oozed innocence, which I wanted to control, and sex appeal, I'm sure she didn't even know she had.

Melanie was by far the most beautiful woman I have ever laid eyes on. And she wasn't even trying. It made me wonder if she knew the allure she had. I wondered if she knew she was damn near bringing me to my knees with her beauty, and possibly had the power to control me opposed to it being the other way around.

Her dark chocolate skin, wild coarse mane, expressive eyes, and full, juicy lips that begged to be kissed and filled with my dick was going to have me losing all my damn control.

I would love to see her on her knees with me submerged between them plump lips, then spilling my seed all over them.

The image had me controlling the body shudder that wanted to move through me.

But my fantasy was quickly shattered as I realized it was one sided.

Melanie rolled her eyes and pursed those sexy ass lips.

"What are you doing here, Warrick?"

I curbed my words because I wanted to tell her what I wanted to do to that smart-ass mouth. Instead, I smiled down at her.

"I came to apologize in person since you won't allow me to do so over the phone. You know, with you ignoring my calls and all."

Melanie smiled.

I inwardly thought that this was going to be much easier

than anticipated. I was for sure she would not forgive me so easily.

"That was thoughtful. Thank you. You have a great evening."

And just like that, my Melanie was back.

My Melanie?

My thoughts took me off guard, because I wasn't thinking of her being mine in the sense of owning her body in the bedroom. That thought crossed my mind with thoughts of her being fully mine.

That shit has never–ever–happened!

That fiery spirit thought... that shit just did something to me.

I wanted to dominate her, but at the same time, I wanted her to continue to give me hell.

Finally, getting out of my head, I laughed at her.

"Don't be like that, Mel. Invite me in."

The way her nipples perked up. I know she wanted to. The question was if she would give in to her body.

She rolled her eyes again, and I think she's really going to send me away, but instead, she huffed loudly and opened the door wider.

I walked through the door, and Melanie headed over to the kitchen.

"You want something to drink?"

Girl, do I?!

I want to drink up all her juices. I can already smell her scent permeating the air, and I don't want any of it to go to waste.

"Come here, Melanie."

A simple command, but my voice is husky and laced with so much promise.

I could tell Melanie also heard the need in my words, but she still proceeded with caution.

"Don't play with me, Warrick. Don't get me all worked up only to command that I am not allowed to come, or that you won't fuck me. That shit is getting old fast."

I let a deep chuckle rumble through me.

She knows what she wants, and I like that.

While I don't have any intentions of making her wait any longer, Melanie still needs to know who is in charge of this shit between us.

And that's me.

I reached out my hand and pulled her to me.

"I promise, baby, no games tonight. You can come as many times as you like. But you still need my permission to do so. You got that?" I said, gazing down at her. "I want to hear you asking for those orgasms. They are mine, and as long as you get permission, I will oblige. Now show me to your bedroom."

Melanie smirked at me, with a hint of defiance in her eyes. But she didn't refuse my request. That let me know she was ready, at least for tonight. The rest, I would slow walk her into.

Melanie's ass jiggled, in what I could now see was a lace G-string, through the sheer fabric of her robe.

A brotha was also turned all the way on by the thought of her walking around her house this way all the time.

Shit. I may need to make that a rule.

When I walked through the entryway of her bedroom and saw the large king-sized four-poster bed, my shit bricked up even harder.

This was perfect for having Melanie bound and splayed, leaving her at my mercy.

"Take off your robe," I commanded.

Melanie surprisingly did as she was told, with no smart remarks falling from her lips. I would be sure to reward her for being such a good girl.

Her long legs were begging to be spread and tied down, with her arms stretched just as wide, but I didn't have any of my shit with me.

Damn. I should have thought ahead.

I had to get creative with what I had. So, I took the sash to her robe, tied her wrists together, and placed them above her head.

"Leave them up there. Don't move your arms, Melanie."

Her response was a low moan in the back of her throat.

I couldn't wait to pry more of those noises from her.

"Warrick," Melanie cried out when I brushed my fingers over her nipple. They were already standing at attention in all their deep chocolate sexiness. Melanie's brown skin was the hue of hazelnut, but her areolas were so damn dark and smooth. They reminded me of freshly melted dark chocolate, and I wanted a taste. I couldn't wait to run my tongue over them–take my time teasing her.

"Yeah, Melanie?" I asked.

"Please don't make me wait any longer. I need to feel you–all of you."

"I'm dying to feel you too, baby."

I stood and removed my shirt, belt, and slacks.

Melanie's eyes followed my every move, and when I stood in front of her in nothing but my briefs, she licked those sexy ass lips. I could tell she wanted to fully take in and taste what was behind the thin fabric.

And my first move–apart from pleasing her–was to give her

what she wanted and allow her to wrap her sexy lips around my dick.

"Melanie, you know by now that I have... different tastes. I need you to know that I'm in control of this—us—when we're in whatever space while I make your body cream. Do you understand that? I need to know before I proceed."

"Yes," she let out breathily.

"Nah, baby. I need you to say it. I want the words."

"Yes, Warrick, you're in control."

Melanie's chest rose with her excited breaths, revealing her desperation for my touch. I could tell the anticipation was getting to her.

Shit, it was getting to me too. And I wanted to touch her just as badly as she wanted to be touched.

"I need a safe word, baby. Because trust me, you will want to tap out, or tell me you can't take anymore. You won't mean it, though. So, what's your safe word, Melanie?"

"Tennessee," she quickly replied.

I chuckled.

"Why Tennessee?"

"That's a place I never want to go again. So, if I say *Tennessee,* that'll let you know you're heading into territory I never want to go."

"I got you, baby."

Now that we got that out of the way, I was going to have some fun with Melanie.

And hopefully, never cause her to use her safe word.

"Let's get you out of these clothes."

I leaned over Melanie and slid her thong over her luscious hips.

On her bedside table was a jar of body butter. Her skin

already looked moisturized and glowing, but I wanted to touch every inch of her. So, I scooped a dollop of the butter into my hand and began to rub along her hips and down her legs.

I kissed as I caressed. And the pleasurable moans that escaped Melanie's lips had me rushing to get to the parts I really wanted... Those lips, and between the soft juncture of her thighs.

Instead of lifting Melanie to get her tank off, I ripped it right down the center.

I needed the contact of her smooth skin, and I didn't want to wait any longer.

Melanie gasped and arched her back, providing the perfect angle to her beautiful breasts and those deep chocolate nipples.

I met her upward thrust with my lips. I took the opportunity to latch onto one nipple, causing her to cry out.

"Warrick, can I please come? Please!"

Melanie was begging and I barely touched her. She was so responsive, and I loved that shit.

Without verbally responding, I slid my hand down to her sweet heat, while maintaining firm sucks to her nipples.

When I reached her pussy, and slid my fingers deep in her center, her tight cavity sucked me in.

Melanie was so wet and tight. And if she was gripping my two fingers with that much intensity, I couldn't wait to feel her warm walls wrapped around my dick.

"I told you all you had to do was ask permission, and I would oblige. Good girl," I praised.

In just a few circular thrusts of my thick digits, Melanie was screaming my name and releasing her honey all over my hand.

"That's it, baby. Ride that wave."

"Warrickkkk!" Melanie cried out.

She brought her tied wrists down and tried to trap me between her bound hands as she burst with pleasure.

"Aht. Aht," I chastised.

I quickly flipped her over and smacked her hard on the ass, twice.

"Ahh!" Melanie cried out in a mixture of pain and pleasure.

"Didn't I say leave your hands above your head?"

I soothed the sting that I knew my slaps left behind. I was going to slow-walk Melanie into the things I liked sexually, but I was also going to make sure she knew I was serious about my rules.

Then, I thrust into her and pulled her hips up off the bed.

The next scream that escaped her lips was one full of ecstasy and probably alerted the neighbors.

"That's right. Take this shit. You said I wasn't properly tending to what was mine, so I'm going take care of this pussy all fucking night."

"Yes, daddy!" Melanie yelled into the pillow she buried her face into.

While most niggas like that *daddy* shit, I never did. In fact, that shit was a major turn-off for me.

I reached my hand out, gripping Melanie by the front of her neck, and pulled her to me, her back flush to mine. I thrust up into her with a hard, punishing thrust.

"Nah, baby. I'm not your daddy. That's not gonna fly with me."

I bit her earlobe, making sure I had her attention.

"I'm your Dom, your Sir, your Master... but never your daddy. You got that shit?"

"Yes, Sir," Melanie moaned.

"Good, girl."

"Can I please come, Sir? I'm so close. I don't think I can hold it any longer."

Damn, she was learning fast, and that shit had my balls drawing tight.

"So, eager, Mel. I'm going to come with you, baby. Wait for me."

"Warrick!" Melanie gasped as my strokes got deeper.

I reached over and stroked her clit between my thumb and forefinger.

Her walls instantly tightened, and I knew I couldn't push her any further–not yet at least.

"Now, Melanie. Come for me, now!" I grunted.

And she did.

I had to hold her body up as I continued to stroke through her orgasm to find my own release.

"Shit, Mel!" I groaned.

I quickly pulled out and spurted my seed all over her ass and back.

I would have loved to spill my seed deep in her walls, but I wasn't trying to make a baby. And I didn't know if she was on birth control.

In our recklessness, we both fell forward, spent from pleasure.

After catching my breath, I got up and headed into the connecting bathroom. I found a washcloth, warmed it under the hot water, and headed to clean Melanie up.

My goal was always to take care of my subs after a scene. And while this wasn't really a scene–probably the most vanilla sex I've had in over a decade–I was still going to tend to Melanie.

I was met with her light snores and chuckled. I saw that I

would have to help her with her stamina. Because what we just did was nothing compared to what I really had in store for her.

Melanie barely moved after I cleaned her up. Only moaned through her snores.

She was so damn adorable.

And while I told her I was going to beat that pussy up all night long, I put my own selfishness aside, and would let her sleep for a little while.

I climbed in the bed, pulled the duvet folded at the bottom of the bed over us, and pulled Melanie close.

I don't think I ever snuggled or cuddled with a woman. It felt foreign, but it also felt good and right.

Chapter Twenty-Two

MELANIE

I woke up and stretched.

My entire damn body felt like I ran a triathlon. I was hurting in places that I didn't even know existed.

But then my mind wandered to the night before and the countless rounds of sex and being controlled by Warrick.

The entire night was something I'd never experienced.

I never knew sex could be so damn good. It definitely was nowhere near this good with Gordon's sorry ass.

Warrick was—he was—shit... I had no words to describe him.

Then, I turned and glanced over at his large sleeping frame beside me.

His arm was draped over my stomach possessively, and the entire moment was... nice.

But I already know not to think too much into whatever this is between us. I'm on the rebound from a terrible marriage, and Warrick is a Dom who needs a submissive. And while I didn't mind being tied up, or curious about more of his sexual tastes...

there isn't a submissive ass bone in my body. Currently, it's all fun. I don't think I could be what he truly needed outside of the bedroom. Albeit, I don't really know what else he expects from a submissive. I guess I have to inquire about that.

Warrick's arm tightened over my belly, but he continued his even breathing, letting me know he was still asleep.

I couldn't hold back my smile.

This was the first time I woke up happy to have a warm manly body next to my own in years.

And I was going to appreciate this for what it was.

Post sated bliss.

Don't get attached though, Melanie. Remember, you're not equipped for his lifestyle.

It was as if my mind was on two different accords. One side, I was enjoying the moment, and the other is being a party-pooping bitch.

Shushing the little Negative Nancy, I relaxed further into the pillow.

I knew I needed to get up and get ready for work, but I closed my eyes anyway.

"Mama! Where you at?! I don't smell coffee."

My eyes popped open and damn near bugged out of my head.

"Shit!" I yelled out, startling Warrick.

"Damn. You're going to give my old ass a heart attack. What's wrong?"

"Naomi is here!" She's supposed to be at Malachi's."

"Mama!" Naomi yelled again, right outside of my door.

Then, she came bursting through my bedroom door. It was normal to burst in on me... it wasn't like I ever had men in my home—in my room. And when I was with Gordon, his ass was gone so often that Naomi took to coming in and jumping in my bed, on his side.

There wasn't enough time to do shit when she came barreling into my room. All I could do was pull the sheets up, covering Warrick and me.

"Shit!" Naomi yelled in shock, covering her eyes, and rushing back out of my room.

"Sorry, Mama! I didn't know you had company."

I groaned.

"What do you want me to do?" Warrick asked.

"Get dressed. I'll go out and do damage control."

He nodded, gathered his clothes, and headed for the bathroom.

I grabbed my robe and headed out to the kitchen, where Naomi was brewing me a cup of coffee.

"I thought you were going to school with Zinae?"

"I left something here that I needed."

I cocked my head because she was being cryptic.

"Yeah? What did you leave? I could have brought it with me to school."

Naomi couldn't look me in the eyes, and now my interest was piqued.

However, she tried to change the subject.

"Sooo... you have a man now?"

"Nope. And back to you... what did you leave home?"

"Umm... promise you won't get mad?"

My heart lurched. And I was worried

What the hell was my baby girl hiding.

"Spit it out, Naomi! Now!"

"My birth control."

"Your what?!" I yelled. "Naomi Brown, you're fucking sixteen!"

How the fuck did I miss this?

Before she could respond, Warrick came strolling into the kitchen in all his sexiness, and my ass was instantly distracted.

"Mel, I'm going to head out. I'll call you later."

He leaned down and gave me a quick kiss on the lips.

Warrick turned to Naomi and gave her a smile and nod.

"Good morning, Naomi."

"Um... good morning Mr. Warrick."

"You ladies have a great day."

When Warrick was out the door, Naomi wasted no time jumping in on me.

"Mama! Mr. Warrick? Uncle Malachi is going to get you!"

"And you're going to keep your big ass mouth shut."

"Only if you promise not to snap on me about my birth control."

"Oh, we're definitely going to talk about that. And you are still going to keep your mouth shut. But right now, I need to get dressed so we can get to school on time."

I poured a cup of coffee and walked back to my bedroom.

When I closed myself in and inhaled, I could still smell Warrick. My pussy did a little flip.

But I had to put all of that out of my mind so that I could figure out why the hell my daughter was sneaking around, taking birth control.

———

Naomi and I piled into my coupe, and I wasted no time goin' in on her.

"Birth control, Naomi? Are you having sex?"

I glared over while Naomi played with a few strands of her curls that escaped her top bun.

I continued to glare when she didn't respond.

"We have twenty minutes until we arrive at school. Don't play with me, little girl!"

Naomi went rigid at my words.

"I'm not a little girl."

Oh, she's definitely having sex, I thought.

Her hot in the pants ass was smelling herself, and I was ready to knock her head between the window and the headrest.

"So, you're grown now? You got a feel of one of these little knucklehead's little wee wee, and you think you can get buck?" I growled, irritated. "At least your ass is smart enough to prevent pregnancy. I hope you're also using condoms to prevent STDs."

"Ugh! This is why I didn't tell you, mama. You be trippin'."

"No, you're trippin' if you think you're mature enough to be having sex. You weren't even woman enough to come and talk to me about it."

"Is that why you're mad? Because I didn't come talk to you?"

I breathed in deep. I didn't want Naomi to feel as if she couldn't talk to me, but damn, I wasn't ready for her to be having sex.

Shit, I wasn't even aware that she had a boyfriend. At least I hoped she was only having sex with one boy.

Oh, Lord! Please don't let my daughter be out here thottin' and shit.

I was also kicking myself for being so wrapped up in my divorce, then the move, then the whirlwind that was Warrick. I felt like shit for allowing Naomi to spend so much time with Malachi and Sinaa. She just seemed so much happier with her sister, so I allowed it.

Thinking of my brother, made me groan at what I knew his reaction would be to Naomi having sex, especially on his watch. He was going to lose his shit.

Interrupting my thoughts, Naomi asked, "Are you like going to put me on punishment?"

"See, that question right there tells me that you're not ready for the road you're traveling, Naomi. But no, I am not going to put you on punishment. You're going to find a way to sneak around anyways. I want to meet this boy, though. Immediately. And that does not mean that you will be free to have sex in my house, or at your uncle's house. I can't stop you because I know I can't, but I will not make it easy for you either. I'm not that mom."

I needed to meet this boy who deflowered my baby. And his parents. Hopefully, they would be on the same page as me and will want to make it hard as possible for them to not be out here fucking like rabbits and getting themselves into some shit they couldn't get themselves out of.

Pulling into the school parking lot, I was already dreading the day because I needed silence to process all that has happened in the last twelve hours, but it looked like I would have to wait another seven to do so.

Thank God for the French Press I put into the teacher's lounge.

I was going to need all the damn coffee today.

I cut the car off and told Naomi to get to class and that we would talk more later.

Now I was going to be on the lookout for any boy she interacted with.

I still couldn't believe that within a few months, she started a new school and found a little boy to take her virginity. At least, I hoped that was something recent and not something she had been doing before we left Tennessee.

"I love you, mama."

"I love you too, my little chocolate drop."

"Ughh! Stop calling me that."

I laughed.

She was my little chocolate drop. Unlike Zinae, she didn't get her dad's cream coffee skin. Naomi's skin glowed dark and smooth like the model Naomi Campbell. She had to get her complexion from my parents because I was dark, but not as dark and lovely as she was.

All this new information about my daughter just made me reflect on so much.

I really didn't have a baby anymore. She'd grown up on me. And I wasn't ready.

Chapter Twenty-Three

MELANIE

The next few weeks I made sure to spend plenty of time with Naomi. I also made it a point to go and check up on all her social media.

With the bomb she dropped on me about her having sex, I felt like I didn't know my daughter, and I didn't want that to be the case. She was my world. And I was going to make sure she knew that.

It was tiring, though. Sixteen-year-olds are so damn hot and cold.

Naomi tried to act like she didn't enjoy our time together, but I knew she did.

We spent afternoons after school going shopping, going to the movies, going out to eat... everything. Zinae even joined in a few times, but Naomi must've told her the deal, because even she stayed away for the most part.

Spending time with both of them had me making sure I brought Sinaa into the loop about everything, just in case Zinae was having sex.

We needed to get these girls off to high school child-free.

Not that they couldn't do both, and be great. It just wasn't the life I wanted for either of them. I wanted them to go to college and experience everything. Hopefully, they would go together and hold one another down while doing so.

I collapsed into bed after a long afternoon of shopping with Naomi. All of the cute little shops could really get somebody in financial trouble. Thanks to Gordon, that wouldn't be my problem. I had plenty of his money to blow.

And Naomi and I have been doing that.

My phone buzzed, breaking my thoughts, and I smiled at Warrick's name on the screen.

I hadn't seen him since that morning he left my condo, but he did call to check on me frequently.

"Hello," I spoke into the phone.

I'm sure he could hear the wide smile on my face.

"Hey, gorgeous. Did you have a good day?"

"I did. How about you?" I countered.

"I did. Thought about you a few times today."

"Oh, yeah? And what were you thinking? Nasty thoughts, probably."

His deep chuckle moved through the speaker into my ear and rocked my senses.

Everything about that damn man was so sexy. And my body was craving him.

Whenever I thought about that night, my pussy would automatically contract as if she were reliving that night's events.

"That. And more."

My skin heated.

I wondered what his freaky ass was thinking. I was curious

about what else he had up his sleeve as far as the whole Dom thing went.

I moaned into the phone.

"Tell me more."

"I'd rather show you."

Shit! I wanted him to show me too, but I wouldn't allow him over here to blow my back out while my daughter was asleep down the hall.

"Naomi's here. Sorry... I'm not ready for her to see a man coming and going from my bed yet."

"That's understandable. And I respect it. But there's more than one way I can show you."

He must've have felt my confused expression because the next thing I know, he hit the FaceTime button.

Thankfully, my ass stayed in sexy night clothes–they made me feel sexy. Otherwise, I would have declined that shit.

I quickly hit the green button, and his gorgeous, deep mahogany skin filled my screen.

Damn, he's so sexy.

"Damn! Do you always lounge around in that sexy ass shit?" He asked, referring to my lavender silk top, with lace trim. The lace barely covered my nipples, and my areolas could be made out through the lace.

I blushed, under his intense scrutiny. And felt pleased at the same time that I appealed to him.

Maybe you are made to be a submissive, Melanie.

That thought caught me off guard because I was sure I was anything but. However, when it came to this man, I was always putty in his hands, doing as he commanded without a second thought. At least after he spanked me on my damn kitchen counter and left me with a dripping pussy.

"Wearing lingerie makes me feel sexy."

"You are without a doubt sexy as fuck, Mel."

I blushed harder.

"Thank you, Warrick."

He winked at me, and honey oozed between my legs.

"Now, take your breasts out of your shirt."

"You want me to just take it off?" I asked.

"Did I tell you to take it off, Melanie?"

And there goes the Dom!

"No, Sir."

"Then do as you're told."

And my ass did! Popping my titties out of my top and letting them fall over the fabric of my nighty.

"You have amazing breasts. I love how dark your areolas are. I can still taste your smooth velvety skin. Play with your nipples for me, Melanie."

With my free hand, I rubbed and pinched each of my nipples. And it felt so damn good.

Somehow with Warrick watching, my breasts felt uber-sensitive. The sensations flowing through my body were way more intense than when I played with my nipples alone, with no audience.

"That's it, baby. Close your eyes. Imagine that I'm there rubbing and sucking on those beautiful nipples."

I couldn't hold back my moan.

I gripped my nipple tighter, almost to the point of pain, and cried out in pleasure. I was about to orgasm from just playing with my nipples.

"Bring that right nipple to your mouth and suck it," Warrick commanded.

I opened my eyes and looked into the camera, making sure I

heard him correctly.

I had never sucked on my own damn nipple before. I didn't even know if it could fit into my mouth.

"Don't question me, Melanie."

His authoritative tone sent shivers down my spine.

"Yes, sir."

I held the phone with one hand, making sure his view wasn't obstructed, and gripped my titty in with my other hand, bringing it to my lips. I took a tentative lick, and it felt so damn weird.

"Don't be shy. Suck that shit."

I opened my mouth, snaked my tongue around my nipple, then closed my lips over it, and sucked hard.

The shit sent lightning bolts straight to my pussy.

"Can I touch myself, Warrick? I'm so close to the edge."

He stared back into the phone, contemplating my words.

"You have something you can prop your phone on? I want to see you spread them thick thighs while you play with your clit."

My ass scrambled off the bed so damn fast, and into my bathroom for my little tripod I use when I'm applying my makeup.

I placed it on my nightstand at the perfect angle and laid in the middle of the bed, facing the phone, making sure Warrick had the view he desired.

My legs fell open and I couldn't control the quick pace of my fingers as they dipped into my honeypot.

"Slow down, baby. There's no rush."

I half groaned, half moaned because I needed the pressure.

But being his *good girl,* I slowed my pace and leisurely stroked my pussy, capturing my lips between my fingers and sliding them back in forth in the slick honey that escaped my hole.

"Shit, Melanie. That's it, baby. Just like that."

Warrick's voice was strained. It sounded like he was gritting the words through his teeth.

I looked up and saw that he had his own phone propped up on something and had pushed himself back from his desk. He was sitting in his office chair, stroking his dick as he watched me.

The vision made my breath catch. No, I take that back... it simply stole the breath straight from my damn lungs. My pants were so loud, and I could feel my heartbeat behind my eardrums.

This entire scene was unlike anything I had ever experienced, and I didn't even come yet.

"Please, sir... can I come?"

"Dip them two fingers inside, stretch that tight hole out for me. And play with your clit with the other hand."

His instructions came out breathily.

I was having the same effect on him, and it turned me on even more.

"Babyyyy! I need to come. PLEASE!"

"That's it. You're doing so good. Let them juices fly, Melanie."

And I did. My body convulsed, and an orgasm so strong wracked my body.

My honey was dripping all down my hand, and I had to pinch my clit to stop the throbbing. That had the opposite effect, though. The pressure only made me leak more.

I looked over at the screen just in time to see Warrick's head fall back against the chair as he groaned my name.

I got closer and picked up the phone.

I watched him stroke his long, thick, veiny dick, and I wanted to dive right back into my honeypot.

"You are so damn sexy," I told him.

Warrick looked back into the camera and our eyes connected.

"Shit. Fuck. Melanie, I'm about to come."

"I wish I was there to catch it."

And with those words, Warrick's semen spurted from his dick on to his stomach, and the sight was so fucking amazing.

When he came down, his hand grabbed something behind his phone, and he came back with a tissue to wipe himself up.

It was quiet for a time. I honestly didn't have the energy to do or say anything.

"You were such a good girl. You're going to be rewarded for that the next time I see you."

I smiled and hummed into the phone.

"Get some sleep, Melanie. I'll call you tomorrow."

I managed a *goodnight*, rolled over and fell asleep. I didn't even give a damn about not cleaning myself up.

Shit, I don't even know if I ended the call. My dreams took me immediately.

———

The next morning, I popped up feeling refreshed and rejuvenated.

Naomi and I drove over to Malachi and Sinaa's house, and I was on cloud nine.

Naomi looked at me funny as I drove, but she didn't say anything. So, I stayed in my happy place–or rather, I stayed in my memories of the night before.

As soon as we arrived at my brother's Naomi went in search of her sister, and I found Sinaa in the kitchen making brunch.

I love Saturdays!

Sinaa always cooked a big brunch on Saturday, and I always loved filling my flabby ass stomach. Sinaa's cooking was not conducive to living a life on Miami Beach. My belly was one waffle away from having to be tucked in a damn moo moo one piece.

"It smells good in here, sis!" I said as I bounced up beside her, taking a peek inside her pots.

"Why you talking in a sing-song voice, all damn happy this morning?"

"No reason, just in a good mood."

She looked me up and down and squinted her eyes.

"You got some, didn't you?! I know a sexually satisfied woman when I see one. Please tell me you finally let Warrick tear that ass up."

I rolled my eyes.

"I have not gotten any... recently. Well, no physical dick. But Warrick did tear my ass up a few weeks ago, and we had the most intense phone sex last night."

Sinaa dropped her spatula and took a seat at the island.

"Tell me more!"

"Girl, you're gonna burn them damn pancakes, and I want them. So, cook while I talk."

She huffed, but climbed off the stool and continued preparing her food.

"Talk, sis!"

I sighed and looked up to the heavens, trying to find words to even describe sex with Warrick.

"Damnnnn! That good? He looks like he knows how to fuck!"

"Sinaa! You're married!"

"And? So what! Am I not supposed to notice a man, and the

way he walks? Because the way Warrick strolls... he's making room for that monster dick he's toting around. It's the same damn walk that Malachi has. And trust me... Malachi has a monster ass dick!"

"First off... GROSS! I do not want to think about my brother's dick. That's just fucking nasty! And second... GIRLLLL... dick so big, I didn't even know how it was going to fit inside of me."

"I knew it!" Sinaa exclaimed all damn loud.

"Shh! I know your husband is somewhere lurking. Be quiet!"

"Girl, some player just got traded to Miami, and Malachi is busy trying to find him a new mansion. He's not worried about us; he's worried about them checks. "

I laughed but was so proud of my brother. He was out here living his dreams, making our parents proud.

I hope they were proud of my behind. Because I truly felt like I was failing them.

Before I could get too deep in my thoughts, Sinaa snapped her hand in front of my face.

"The dick was that good?!"

I smacked her hand away.

"It was, but I was thinking about other things in life."

"Nahh... you can sidetrack later. Right now, I wanna know what that dick do."

I rolled my eyes.

She was acting as if she were dicked deprived, and I knew she wasn't... I shared a house with her and my brother.

But I couldn't help but to be pulled into the excitement.

"Girl, he is into some serious BDSM shit. I don't even know, really. All I know is that the first time he came to take me out on a date, and I opened the door naked, he spanked me for disobeying him. Then he's always giving out commands like, *you have to ask permission before coming.* Then he tied me up with my robe sash and fucked the entire shit out of me. Warrick had me dizzy from a sex-induced haze by the time he was finished with me. I don't even know how to digest it all."

"I know how... in your damn mouth!"

We both fell out in a fit of giggles.

"Girl, I don't even know if I will be able to take it all down."

"Damnnnn... he packing like that?"

"I tell no lies... pinky swear."

"You tell no lies about what?" Malachi asked as he walked his annoying self into the kitchen.

"Nothing."

"Y'all lying," he accused.

"Then what you ask for, dummy?" I said to him.

"I heard y'all talking about Warrick. Melanie, didn't I tell your ass to stay away from him. And Si, really? You gon' make me fuck you up in here wanting details of another man's dick."

"Aww, baby... don't be jealous! Your dick is the only dick I want."

I had to watch Sinaa strut over to Malachi and grab on his junk through his sweatpants.

I was so disgusted.

Malachi smacked her hand away, but pulled Sinaa closer and squeezed her ass.

"Yeah, okay. Don't play with me, Si."

"Can y'all get a damn room? I am standing right here."

"I don't have to get shit. This is my house," Malachi retorted.

"I really hate your big, block head ass sometimes. Ugh!"

Malachi pulled away from Sinaa and sucked his teeth.

"Whatever. Just stay the fuck away from Warrick, Mel."

"Nigga, bye!"

Once Malachi was out of the room, Sinaa looked over at me and shrugged.

"I say do you, boo! I'm not sure why he's so mad."

"Because apparently he knows a little about Warrick's life-style, and I guess he doesn't want to think of me being mixed up in it."

"Shiddd. I might go to the store and buy us some cuffs and shit. I'm tryna see what it's hitting for."

"You're a got-damn fool, Sinaa. Hurry up and finish this damn breakfast. I'm hungry!"

We all feasted on the spread Sinaa laid out and made small talk.

Malachi seldomly gave me dirty looks because he now knew I was involved with Warrick. Disdain was written all over his face, and Sinaa tried to ease the tension between us.

I could give two shits about what he thought.

While I didn't want to beef with my brother, he was just going to have to accept the fact that I was grown, and could make my own decisions.

And right now, I wanted to explore a physical relationship with Warrick, no matter what he thought or said.

And I wasn't going to let him mess up me pigging out on all of this delicious food.

He'll be okay.

Chapter Twenty-Four

WARRICK

A few weeks had gone by, and I hadn't seen Melanie.

My body was craving her like an addict.

I understood that she needed to spend time with her daughter, though.

I had my own twin girls that needed my sole attention every so often, because they always thought the moment I got busy that they could sneak and do whatever the hell they wanted.

Regardless, I still wanted Melanie, and I hoped to get a fix of her soon.

My schedule had been hectic with the football season in full effect, but that didn't stop me from envisioning Melanie's thick, luscious thighs spread out before me.

Get a hold of yourself, War!

I had never let a submissive distract me from my job. I loved what I did, and in addition to my fucked-up past, it was probably another reason I could never accept the fact that I wasn't the relationship type.

Blasting some old school rap music, I tried to get back in my zone and look over the upcoming week's matchup schedule. There were four division games, so I knew Sunday was going to be live.

I needed to make sure I had enough material prepared so that I could have all the points, sarcastic comments, and players of the week ready in my arsenal to keep my viewers entertained.

It was good enough to just broadcast about just the game any longer. I had to know what players were beefing, causing the team to be out of sync, what players were fucking up off the field, what coaches were in the hotseat, etcetera etcetera. Putting together a fully packed and entertaining show was hard work.

But I loved every minute of it.

I'd love it even more if I had some pussy right about now.

And there went my thoughts.

The rap music wasn't helping me currently, so I decided to take a break and call Melanie.

She picked up just as I thought the phone was going to go to voicemail.

"Hello," her raspy voice came through the speakerphone.

"Did I wake you?" I asked, and looked over at the clock. I didn't realize how late it was.

"Yeah, but it's okay. I was doing more tossing and turning than I was actual sleeping."

That had me interested.

I wondered if she was up thinking about me just as I was her.

"Why couldn't you sleep, Melanie?"

I put my dominant voice on, letting her know not to lie to me.

When I talked a certain way, my submissives could never

refuse to fully answer. It was as if the power in me called to the power in them. And I say *power* because it took a powerful woman to be a submissive. Most people thought submissives were weak, but it was quite the opposite.

To allow someone to fully have control over your body took control only one with power wielded. And I loved every minute of it.

I wasn't quite sure yet if Melanie was a submissive, but so far, she did a good job at allowing me to dominate her body.

I had to wonder, though... if she became my full time submissive, would she allow me control over all things?

I didn't think she was ready for that. I wouldn't push all of that on her yet.

So far, she enjoyed allowing me to take full control over her body. Naturally, she wants to give me power over all things.

That made my dick twitch.

"I was thinking about you."

I smiled.

Good girl.

I was pleased she openly told me the truth.

"What were you thinking?" I asked.

"About how I don't want my brother to try to kill you after finding out we are involved."

Now, that took me by surprise. I knew Malachi didn't want me anywhere near Melanie, but I also told him to mind his business.

I see now that he's going to be a problem. And I really didn't want that.

Because I was going to have Melanie.

"Don't worry about Khi. He'll be okay."

"He thinks that I can't handle you."

Shit. I'm not convinced either.

I didn't speak those words out loud, though.

I wanted Melanie to make up her own mind.

"I think you can. And I think you'll love every second of it. In fact, let me show you how much you'll enjoy being in my world. Come to my house this weekend. I have so much more to show you."

"Oh really? I can't wait."

"I will test you, Melanie. Know that. I know you've probably read books, and watched movies and shit. But being in a scene, giving up control, allowing yourself to feel pain... it will be real. Also, know that I'm am not a Dom who gets off on only inflicting pain. I enjoy straddling that line of pleasurable pain. My ultimate goal, will always be to take care of you and make you feel good."

"What kind of pain?" Melanie asked, a little hesitant with her words.

"It's better if I show you. Come over Friday night."

"Okay."

"I'm going to let you go because if I listen to your sexy ass voice for another minute, I'm going to order you to come over here right now, so I can tie your ass up and have my way with you."

"Goodbye, Warrick," Melanie said breathily.

I had to chuckle because I knew she was wet and ready for me with just my words.

"Goodnight, Melanie. Make sure you get some proper sleep this week. And eat healthy, balanced meals, and stay hydrated. You're gonna need all your energy. You understand?"

"Yes, sir," she whispered.

"Good girl."

I hung up the phone, because my brain and dick couldn't take anymore.

I wanted to bend Melanie over, tie her up, spank her, and shove my dick deep in all her holes.

Dammit, War... you have a show to get together!

Chapter Twenty-Five

MELANIE

Finally, Warrick invited me over to his place. And I couldn't contain my excitement. The little glimpses into his world have left me intrigued and wanting more.

"Make yourself at home, Mel," he told me as he led me into the huge modern house.

It was breathtaking. The entire back wall was floor-to-ceiling windows, with an amazing view of the water beyond the glass. The living areas were huge and open. Warrick's decor was modern, and manly, yet held class.

His home was way more than I could take in at a quick glance, but my body hummed for him. Not his house.

And the way he called me Mel...

I know I may have been overthinking it, but it felt so intimate. Like his tongue was caressing over the one syllable as if he would my body.

I turned to him and gave him a knowing look.

In turn, Warrick let a deep chuckle rumble from his chest.

"So impatient, baby."

I blushed. Because shit... I was impatient.

The way Warrick owned my body that night he popped up at my door apologizing, had me ready for more. The way he caught me off guard, using my robe sash to bind my wrists... it was so damn hot.

Don't even get me started on the phone sex we had. That shit was... electric!

My pussy leaked just from the thought.

So yeah, my impatient ass wanted more of that shit.

I must have been in my head for too long. Because Warrick pulled out a stool at the island and commanded that I sit.

He went into the wine fridge on the side of the island and pulled out what looked like an expensive bottle of wine.

After pouring a nice-sized portion for the both of us, Warrick took a seat next to me.

"How was your day?"

Is he really asking about my damn day when my honey pot is oozing all onto the seat of my lace-clad panties?

"I teach high school kids... so you can imagine," I said with a chuckle. "Some good stress relief would be good."

"So eager."

"Warrick, stop playing with me. You know why I'm here. And it ain't to claim a drawer and leave a toothbrush on your bathroom counter."

The way his smile spread across his face, showcasing those perfect white teeth, against the dark fullness of his beard... pussy gone! That thang done jumped from between my legs, directly into Warrick's possession.

And he knew it too.

But his ass continued to ignore me.

"That mouth," was all he said, then asked if I wanted food. "You hungry? You need some food with your wine? I don't want you to get an upset stomach."

I rolled my eyes.

"I had a big lunch. Thanks. Plus, you commanded that I eat properly leading up to tonight."

"I'm glad you are having no problems doing as you are told. I'll make sure you're rewarded for your obedience. However, I'm trying to have a nice evening with you, Melanie. You know... dinner, stimulating conversation... all of that."

"But why? We're just having fun... good ole nasty fun."

Warrick laughed hard. The sound was so loud it reverberated off the walls.

I crossed my arms over my chest, looking back at him, annoyed.

"What's so damn funny?"

"You are."

"Don't mock me. You told me a Dom/Sub relationship was what you had to offer, and that's what I'm coming to give you. Don't wine and dine me."

"Believe it or not, Melanie, when I have a submissive outside of the club, which is rare, but it has occurred, I treat her with the utmost respect and take good care of her. So, if you are going to accept me as your Dom, know that you will be taken care of."

Damn. That sounded good. I've never had a man tell me that he was going to take care of me. Not even Gordon, he basically found out I was pregnant and said, *we have to get married.* And his ass definitely didn't take care of me... my mind, my body, or my spirit.

But could I allow Warrick to take care of me as his submissive and not fall in love with him? Not want more from him?

Shit, I hope I can. Because I already wanted him to take care of me sexually. And I knew I was going to give in to his will.

That thought had me questioning whether I was weak or not.

I may have grown up in the heavy crime-ridden streets of New York, but I lost who I was somewhere along the way to this very moment, and I didn't quite feel like that young woman who wouldn't hesitate to pull the Timbs on and get the Vaseline out.

I really felt weak, and the epiphany was shocking me to my core at the moment.

"Baby, where did you go?"

Warrick's coaxing tone forced me to get out of my head, and my past.

"Just thinking about my life and how weak I had to become to really allow myself to become someone's submissive."

He was out of his seat with quickness.

Pulling me to him, Warrick gripped the back of my neck—hard— and pulled my head up so that our eyes could connect.

I almost came right there on the spot. I knew he could probably smell the scent of my arousal because I could smell it.

"Melanie, don't ever fucking call yourself weak. You understand me? I will not allow that shit."

I nodded, but I guess that wasn't good enough for Warrick.

His ass gripped my neck tighter, and pulled at the hair at the base of my neck.

The shit hurt, but it also left a rush of pleasure in its wake.

"You understand, Melanie?"

"Yes, Warrick. I understand," I told him.

"Good girl."

He leaned down and took my lips in his, sucking hard on my bottom lip. I could already feel it plumping up from his assault.

He was in total control of the kiss; all I could do was hold on for the ride. I knew he was asserting his dominance and letting me know not to go against him.

"And Melanie," Warrick said when he parted from my lips, "Submissives are more powerful than their Doms. You hold all the power, baby. It takes courage, strength, and a level of trust most people don't possess to allow someone else to dominate them. And as your Dom, I can only do what you allow. The moment you let Tennessee slip from your lips, everything stops. You have the power, baby. Never forget that."

I heard everything he was saying, but my brain, and vagina, was still stuck on the grip he had on my neck, causing currents to travel straight to my pussy.

"Since I have all of the power, can you take me to your dungeon, playroom, or whatever you call it?"

My favorite sound escaped Warrick's lips.

His chuckle just did something to me. It was so deep and sexy.

"Come on, girl, before I have to punish your ass for being a pain in *my* ass."

Warrick picked me up and threw me over his shoulder. He ran up the large stairway as I squealed.

He smacked me hard on the ass.

"Quiet. Now!"

Shit, my kitty was purring for this big ass man.

But I bit down on my lip, doing as I was told.

My ass shut right the fuck on up.

I like when Warrick called me a good girl and rewarded me with pleasure.

I've only been disobedient once. I had a feeling that the spanking he gave me on my ass, pushing me to the brink of release, only to pull me back, was only the tip of the iceberg of the punishments he had in his pocket.

Stopping in front of what looked to be a bedroom door. Warrick placed me on my feet and pulled a key out of his pocket, unlocking the door.

He has to keep his little sex dungeon locked. That's interesting.

"Why the locks?" I asked.

"Mea and Mya–they get enough shit surrounding speculation of my sex life. They don't need to see any of this shit."

"Gotcha. Naomi would have a field day with this shit."

I was thinking about the horrified expression that would grace Naomi and Zinae's face if they even found out this shit.

But then my own face took on a horrified expression, because what I imagined didn't even come close to what I took in when Warrick opened the door.

The first thing I saw was a big ass X-looking cross. My ass wanted to shit myself.

My fear caused Warrick to get a slight gleam in his eye. That scared me even more.

Oh, this muthafucka is really about to hurt my ass. Fucking run, Melanie. Now!

However, my feet wouldn't listen to my brain.

Instead, my stupid ass walked further into the room, investigating shit.

It was like my ass was a stupid ass white girl in a scary movie... just waiting to be the fuck murdered.

Warrick allowed me access, and stayed standing against the door frame of the entryway.

My stupid ass walked even further into the room and right up to the damn cross, rubbing my fingers along the surface. It felt like metal, covered in a plush navy silk covering. The sides had all types of loops and ties and whatnot for restraints.

Once my curiosity was indulged with that, I did a little spin and took in the rest of the room.

I was surprised that it wasn't cloaked in deep dark reds or black. I envisioned some type of dungeon-looking shit. Even though that damn X was really giving me some Roman Empire ass vibes, the rest of the room was very inviting. The navy blues and whites didn't make me feel like I was about to be on some shit... but my mind knew better.

"It's different from what I pictured."

"Stop watching T.V. This is my version of a playroom. Dominance doesn't have to be dark."

"Oh." I ain't know what else to say. My nerves were starting to take over.

"Melanie."

I jumped. Warrick was right there, behind me, and I could feel his breath on my ear.

"A few rules..." He said, and trailed off.

He looked down at me, making sure he had my full attention.

I stared back at him, unblinking.

"One—I am always Sir or Master here. Never Warrick. Two—I own all of your pleasure. Every orgasm... your body... your pussy... it is all mine to do with as I please. Which takes me to rule number three. I will never repeat a command. Unless you are using your safe word, do what I say the first time being told. Four—consequences for disobedience... I take them very seriously. So, I suggest you don't try me. But I have a feeling it may take you a little while to control that mouth of yours. But don't worry... I'll have something for that.

My fifth and final rule—no fucking clothes on in this room.

You cross this threshold; you need to be naked before I enter the room. If you think I'm right behind you, you better start undressing in the damn hallway, up the stairs... wherever—just be naked and ready for me."

"You understand my rules?"

"Yes, Sir."

My chest was heaving up and down. I was so turned on—and scared. The rush of endorphins had me hot, yet shivering at the same damn time.

"If you understand, why aren't you removing your clothes? I told you the rules—follow them. No clothes."

Again, I jumped.

The base Warrick put in his voice scared the shit out of me.

What the fuck you get yourself into, Melanie?

But guess what my ass did?

I slipped my dress over my head, stepped out of my shoes, slid my panties down, and finished with removing my bra.

"Fucking beautiful."

I felt awkward, even though Warrick had seen me naked, and we had already had sex.

Warrick removed his button-up shirt and belt, before undoing the button on his slacks. He didn't remove them, though.

He was so damn sexy. His broad chest, and wide shoulders were absolutely drool worthy. I wanted to touch him so bad. But I wasn't sure if I could. There were no rules regarding me touching him.

"Can I touch you? Sir."

I almost forgot his first damn rule just that fast.

"Not right now."

Warrick turned me around, held my hands behind my back, and walked me over to the foot of the bed.

He gently pushed my back down causing my breasts and stomach to be flush with the mattress. The cool silk had my nipples pebbling on contact.

I had to encourage myself to breathe. Warrick was behind me, and I didn't know what he was doing. His grip was still firm on my wrists, so at least I knew he was still right behind me.

I almost jumped off the bed when I felt his snake across my ass cheeks.

"I didn't think you would be able to be still. We're going to work on that. But for now..." He trailed off.

Next thing I knew, he had one hand bound to the four-poster bed, attached something to it, then encircled the extension around my waist, strapped me in, then finally bound my other hand. The shit around my waist was reminiscent of a waist trainer around my midsection, with rope attached spreading my arms as wide as they could go.

I was the hell confused.

Once Warrick had me locked in, he went back to licking and sucking on my ass. When his tongue trailed down the crack of my ass, I wanted to jump off the fucking bed. But of course, I couldn't. I had never had a man lick my ass, and the shit felt weirdly amazing.

"Warrick!" I cried out.

Smack!

He brought his hand down hard on my ass, and held on to what I assumed was a loop or some type of grip on the back of the contraption he had me in.

Warrick yanked me down as I instinctively tried to maneuver away from his slap.

Oh, that's what this is for.

"Who am I in this room, Melanie?" He asked, giving one more hard smack on the ass.

This time though... his long fingers landed right against my center and I orgasmed. I was so worked up I couldn't hold it any longer. My body was just going through so much. I was having a sensory overload moment.

Warrick tisked.

"You've broken two of my rules in the first ten minutes, Melanie. What should I do with you?"

Fuck!

Chapter Twenty-Six

WARRICK

I was going to love making Melanie's skin tinge pink. It would be a feat as her smooth skin glowed the most magnificent tone of mahogany, but I was up for the challenge.

She needed to know that I took my rules seriously. Especially behind these doors.

"Did I give you permission to come, Melanie? Did you even utter the request?"

"No, Sir. But I couldn't hold it."

"You will learn—starting right now."

"Please don't punish me, Sir. I'm still learning."

"This will give you the motivation you need to keep my rules at the forefront."

I left from behind her and went to retrieve one of my floggers. The one I chose was made of the softest leather, but on the ends of the tassels were little spikes. It definitely left a sting on contact, but used right, it could intensify pleasure.

"Baby, I need you to breathe."

Melanie stiffened.

"And relax. Know that your pleasure is my number one priority... but on my terms."

Melanie did as she was told and relaxed her upper body into the mattress. Her feet were still planted on the floor with her legs spread wide.

I got a perfect view of her pretty pussy lips, and my dick wanted to jump out and claim her.

I learned to become a patient man. It was needed to maintain the level of control I strived to, but Melanie seriously altered all of that for me. And I currently wasn't doing too well with not burying myself deep inside of her.

I stared back at Melanie's pussy, trying to ignore the way her juices were calling to me, commanding me to lick them up. Breathing in deep had the opposite effect I wanted it to, because my nostrils were assailed with the sweet aroma of her scent.

Regaining my control, and composure, I was glad that Melanie couldn't see my face. If she was able to see the true power she had over me, I know her smart mouth ass would try to reverse our roles, and coax me to lessen her punishment.

"Arrggh!" Melanie cried out when the flogger connected with her bare ass.

"You know your safe word, right?"

"Yes, Sir. Tennessee, Sir."

I smoothed my hand over her cheek, rubbing away the sting I knew the connection with the flogger left behind.

"Good girl."

I landed another swing to her other ass cheek, but didn't allow much time for her to recover. My third swing landed right in the middle of her cheeks, and the spikes connected with her leaky pussy.

"Sir, can I please come? I need to feel you."

"No, you cannot. You don't tell me what you need in this room. I already know. You understand?"

Her voice was quivering, and she shook her head up and down.

I made contact with her center again, causing Melanie to moan. The sound was music to my ears. And I knew she wanted to come.

"I can't hear you."

I stroked her center, rubbing her honey all over her lips and her tight puckered hole for lubrication.

"Yes, Sir. I understand."

"Why are you being punished, Melanie?"

Before she could answer, I slipped a plug in her tight hole and rubbed her clit.

Her legs were shaking, and I knew she wouldn't be able to take much more, but I wanted to push her limits. She needed me to build up her stamina.

"Because I called you by your name, and because I came without permission."

"Will you do it again?" I asked as I continued to stroke her with my middle finger.

Her hands pulled against the restraints, trying to get away, but there wasn't anywhere for her to go.

"No, Sir."

She was learning fast.

And my dick was so hard that it hurt. I needed to put us both out of our misery.

I dropped the flogger, shoved my pants down, and plummeted into Melanie's hot, tight core in one long thrust.

Her feet went slack, and I had to pull her up by the waist strap I had her harnessed in.

Leaning over her, I whispered in her ear, "Take all of this dick, Melanie. Don't run."

All I got was whimpers and moans in response.

I began steady thrusts, and the way her muscles tightened around me, I knew she was going to come.

"Can I please come? I don't want to disappoint you, but I don't think I can hold it any longer."

Her words came out shaky and whiny. But I was proud of the control she was attempting to garner.

I clicked the button on the butt plug and sped up my thrust.

"Yes. Come with me, Melanie."

That was all she needed. Her release oozed out of her and coated my dick and pelvis.

I let out a loud groan of my own before pulling out and spurting my seed all over her back.

Melanie went limp under me. She was spent and I knew it.

I reached over to undo her restraints and scooted her all the way up on the bed.

I pulled her into my arms, stroked her hair, and whispered how good she did.

The Dom in me was sated, but the man in me never wanted her to leave my embrace, and that was a feeling unlike anything I've felt.

Melanie was exhausted and it took no time for her to fall into a deep slumber.

Meanwhile, I held her in my arms, wide awake, looking up at the ceiling. I needed to figure out what these feelings meant. Because I was ready to break my own self-imposed rule.

Never fall for your sub, War.

As the thought entered my brain, I was convinced it was already too late.

The sweet innocence in Melanie was unlike anything I had ever experienced. Especially in a woman who was approaching forty.

I couldn't wait to teach her so much more about my world. And hopefully controlled myself from slipping into hers.

Chapter Twenty-Seven

MELANIE

I woke up feeling like Warrick and I played a game of football instead of having sex.

My entire body ached.

But it was a good ache, though.

Warrick woke me up in the middle of the night, and surprisingly sexed me good ole vanilla style in the bed.

I didn't know what he was thinking while he tenderly stroked me, but it felt like how a man would sex on the love of his life.

He made my body feel treasured.

And when he turned me over to lay on my stomach, he rubbed away the soreness I felt on my ass cheek from the flogger, then encased my body between his thighs and slow stroked me into orgasm after orgasm, telling me that I could come as much as I wanted.

The way in which he took care of my body was unlike anything I ever experienced, and it caused tears to fill up behind my lids.

I hoped he thought it was just from the overwhelming plea-sure, because I did not need him to know how much of an emotional wreck I really was.

After he finished loving me up, Warrick carried me into the en suite bathroom and ran me a nice hot bath. He sat beside the tub and cleaned my body. Then he pulled me up and ran a warm shower where he joined me, washing me again, and washing himself.

I thought we were going to settle back into the bed, but he surprised me again, carried me to his bedroom and gently laid me down after pulling back the duvet.

I had no problems falling back to sleep, wrapped tightly in his arms.

The shit was confusing, but I told myself that I would deal with it another day. Because my brain couldn't take anything else.

The next morning, I woke up, and Warrick was staring down at me with a weird expression on his face.

I rubbed the sleep out of my eyes, and covered my mouth before saying, "Good morning."

He smiled down at me.

"Good morning, beautiful. Did you sleep well?"

"Yes, Sir."

"We are in my bedroom; you don't have to call me sir."

"Okay."

We laid in silence a little while longer, and my mind started racing with a bunch of questions about his life.

I felt like I knew Warrick, but at the same time, I didn't.

Maybe he'll tell you about himself, I thought.

"Why do you like BDSM?"

Shit, just right to it, huh? My brain was really on one this morning.

"I was abused as a kid."

Well, damn... I didn't really think he was going to answer. I stared back at him, schooling my expression, because I knew the last thing he would want would be my pity.

So, I just stroked his arm, encouraging him to continue.

"My parents physically abused me. Then I was taken from them and put in the care of my grandparents at twelve, only to endure more abuse."

"So, you like to inflict pain because it was inflicted on you?"

"Not really. I don't see it that way. I like control. I like rules. And there has to be consequences for not following the rules. I don't do it because I want to inflict the pain that was done to me onto others. My pleasure comes from giving pleasure, with boundaries. I need boundaries because so many people in my life have crossed lines that should have never even been encroached upon as a child."

"Oh. Okay. I guess I understand. So is love like a hard limit for you?"

"*Hard limit?* You've been doing your research, I see."

"I did a little. I had to know what I was getting into."

"Love was a hard limit for me."

"Was?" I asked, curiously.

"Yes. I'm not so sure about that now. But that's enough about that. Do you want some breakfast? I'm sure you're hungry."

I allowed him to change the subject. I could tell that this topic wasn't an easy one for him and I wouldn't push.

"I could definitely go for a gourmet breakfast with some fresh-squeezed orange juice. Oh, and don't forget the coffee."

Warrick chuckled.

I swear I was falling in love with the sound.

"You're so beautiful," he responded.

I didn't know what to say, and I'm sure if I were lighter, my cheeks would give away my blush.

"I can make all of that happen. Whatever you want, Melanie, you got it."

"Well, in that case..."

I slid down under the covers.

"How about I start with the best vitamins out there?"

We weren't inside his playroom, so I didn't think he would be opposed to a little morning head.

And the sound that left Warrick's lips with my tongue made contact with the tip of his dick, confirmed that he did not have a problem with it.

He did pull back the sheet so he could watch.

The first few glides of my mouth, Warrick let me control the pace. But as soon as I had enough saliva to effortlessly bob up and down, he gathered my hair at the base of my neck and took over my movements.

He fucked my mouth like he did my pussy, and I was getting so wet.

"Them fucking lips! I've been wanting them lips on my dick since the day I laid eyes on you. They are so plump and sexy. So perfect. Just right to be wrapped around my dick. Mmm... shit. Suck that shit just like that. Let me feel the back of your throat, baby."

Warrick coached me how he liked his dick to be sucked and praised my efforts to fit all of him in my mouth.

His girth was so heady that I couldn't even wrap my full around his dick. I had to use both hands and stroke him up and down as I glided as much of him as I could into my mouth.

When he started fucking my face faster, I tightened my suction and firmly wrapped my lips around the tip of his dick, while continuing to stroke the base of him.

"Melanie. Damn. I'm coming. You gonna swallow that?"

I didn't even waste time with a verbal response.

I slid him deeper down my throat and wiggled my head from side to side, making sure the tip of his dick massaged the back of my throat.

And just like that, I felt bursts of come fill my mouth.

I swallowed every last damn drop.

Warrick threw his head back into the pillow, catching his breath.

Next thing I know, he hauled my ass up and sat me on his face.

"Ride my face, Melanie. Ride that shit like you would my dick."

I ain't never ride a man's face before, but at thirty-eight, I guess there was a first time for everything.

Because if I knew one thing about Warrick so far, he did not like to be disobeyed. And who in their right mind would be disobedient to commands of pussy eating.

Not my ass.

So, I shook off my nerves of smothering him to death, and rode the fuck out of his face.

———

Monday morning blues weren't a thing for me as I walked into the teacher's lounge. I was on a high like no other. My body felt relaxed, and my mind was at ease.

Too at ease, if I really thought about it.

I stayed with Warrick until midday Sunday, and he fucked my body in and out of his playroom. We lounged around, watched T.V., and pigged out on takeout.

The time we spent together had my heart feeling with unknown emotions.

But now that I was back in my own space, I had to coach myself to keep my shit together and my feelings in check. Because if I wasn't careful, I would end up falling for Warrick's ass.

Even though he treated me like a girlfriend this past weekend, and not just a submissive.

From my research, I knew every Dom/Sub relationship was different, but the way he massaged my feet, fed me from his plate, and fucked me slow in his bed, had me feeling like a regular woman being taken care of by a regular man.

However, I was not about to become one of those women who thought they could change a man. And quite frankly, I still felt like I was too fragile to let the first man I let sex me down after a rough divorce play with my heart.

But I was still going to enjoy this moment of bliss.

Warrick even texted me this morning, telling me that he hoped I had a great day.

I left the teacher's lounge with a tall mug of fresh, hot coffee and went to get settled into my first class, broke out my Black History flashcards, and planned a fun and interactive review before quarterly tests took place.

Naomi and Zinae were the first students to arrive.

After testing me a few times with their tardiness, they made sure to be prompt to my class. And I had to admit, I enjoyed them in my space before the other students filed in.

"Hi, mama! I missed you this weekend."

I gave her ass the side-eye because the tracker on her phone let me know that she kept busy. And she snuck off to see her little boyfriend.

I knew I couldn't lock her ass away, but I truly wanted to. Especially after meeting the little ninja that she was dating. That boy looked like a grown ass man, standing over six feet tall with dreads. I was just praying that little BIG boy didn't knock my damn daughter up.

"Hi, baby. Hi, Zinae. How was y'all weekend?"

"It was good Aunt Mel. Even though this one here left me all of Saturday."

"Dang, Zinae. You didn't have to rat me out like that," Naomi whined.

"Little girl, I already knew what you were doing and where you were. All I know is that you better remember that you're only sixteen years old, and don't test the freedom that I give your ass. Because I can and will take it away if you get beside yourself."

"Yes, ma'am."

"Zinae, teach your sister how to be about them books, and to stay out of these little ninjas' faces."

Zinae laughed and shrugged.

"I'll try, Aunt Mel."

Naomi sucked her teeth.

"Both of y'all get on my nerves."

I laughed and went back to preparing for my class as more students filed in.

Class went by in a breeze, and so did most of the day.

But when I finally settled down and checked my personal emails, everything went to shit.

I had an email from Vanessa letting me know that Gordon

had filed a Petition for Contempt. I was mind blown. His petition was pages upon pages of accusations that I was keeping
Naomi from him. That shit was absolutely not true. His stupid
ass had missed three consecutive weekends with Naomi, and she
didn't want to be bothered. I couldn't make the girl go spend
time with her dad. She was too old for me to force her.

I called Vanessa after I calmed down, and she answered her
cell on the first ring.

"You've got to be shittin' me, Vanessa. Really?"

"I know, Melanie. I'm sorry that he won't just go crawl under
a rock and let you live."

"What's the best/worst-case scenario?"

"Well, being as though Naomi has not seen her father since
she left Tennessee, you can be held in contempt and forced to
pay his attorney fees. Best case scenario, we can show proof that
he's blown several visitation times, and that Naomi was hurt.
Also, we can play on the fact that now that she is getting settled
into her new life, she doesn't want to disrupt that. Seldom will a
judge let a minor testify, but I may be able to pull some strings if
Naomi wants to. However, that could also backfire, and the
judge could order reunification therapy."

I groaned.

This cannot be my life!

"Do what you have to do. But I am not paying his attorney's
fees, Vanessa. First of all, it damn sure did not take fifteen thousand dollars to file this damn document."

"I agree. But you'll have to come to Clarington in two weeks
for the hearing. Send me all copies of communication that he
has had with you and Naomi since the divorce was final."

"I can do that. Thank you for your help."

"I got you, girl! And as soon as I take a vacation, I am

coming to see you, so we can chill out at the beach and watch some eye candy stroll by all day. Lord knows I need a man."

I laughed.

Vanessa was beautiful. Tall, slim, cream-colored skin, long thick black hair, and a style that could rival the fliest celebrities.

"Come on, girl."

"I'm there. That brother of yours have any sexy ass friends?"

I thought of Warrick, and smiled.

"I only know one. But he's off-limits, But I'm sure he has others."

"Ohhhh… look at you… *he's off-limits,* huh? Let me find out you done moved to Miami and got some new dick."

I couldn't hold back my girly giggles. It felt good to be having some girl talk with someone other than Sinaa. I knew she wouldn't tell my brother too much about the things I told her, but she was still his wife, and I'm sure they pillow talked. The last thing I wanted was for Malachi to know intimate details about Warrick and me. With Vanessa, I didn't feel like I had to worry about that.

"Girl, you wouldn't believe some of the shit if I told you about Warrick. He is just a different type of breed. And I'm not even sure I can handle him, but I'm giving it a try."

"Well, you sound happy, and I love it. Keep doing you, and let me handle your no-good ex-husband."

"I trust you. I'll see you in two weeks."

We ended the call, and I packed my things up for the day.

Naomi had drama club, but I would wait around for her, because I didn't see her all weekend. Also, I didn't want her to think she could run off to that little boy's house on a damn school night.

Ugh! What am I gonna do with this little girl?!

More importantly, what the hell was I going to do with Gordon's trifling ass.

MEN!

My new, feel-good attitude was striped just that quickly—reminding me that men ain't shit.

Chapter Twenty-Eight

WARRICK

Melanie went radio silent on me after our combustible weekend together, and I was a little confused.

I tried calling her a few times, but she was short with me. When I attempted to take her out to dinner, she declined, using the fact that it was a school night as an excuse.

I didn't want to pull my dominance card, but it was now Thursday, and I hadn't talked to her much since Sunday. I wanted to hear her voice, see her beautiful face. Feel her soft, ample curves under my palms.

My feelings for her were spiraling way past what they should.

And they had me on some sucker shit.

Because here I stood, on the outside of her door, trying to talk myself into walking away.

But I couldn't.

So, instead of walking away, I knocked.

Naomi answered the door with a look of surprise on her face.

"Um, hi Mr. Warrick."

"Hi, Naomi. Is your mother here?"

"Yeah, hold on."

She turned, and left me standing in the doorway. Naomi walked away, leaving the door open, so I headed inside and closed the door.

Melanie came out in a long navy-blue silk robe, tied at the waist. But I could see the deep blue lace of her bra peeking out of the opening in her robe.

I knew it was a kid around, so I told my dick to settle down.

"What are you doing here?"

There was no welcoming tone in Melanie's voice, and it left me wondering if I did something wrong.

"You good? I was just coming to check on you, because I haven't been able to get in contact with you."

"Yeah, I'm fine," she answered dryly.

"You sure? Because your tone and body language say something different," I accused.

"Did you ever think I just didn't feel like talking, Warrick? It has been a long week, and I don't feel like playing your little game."

Whoa! What the fuck?!

I walked closer to her. I knew I couldn't punish her the way I wanted, but she would still know not to come at me like in the manner she did.

Filling her personal space, I leaned down, making eye contact with Melanie.

"Excuse me? Watch your mouth, Melanie."

"I don't have to watch shit. I'm playing this game. All you niggas want to do is have control. Well, I'm tired of being controlled. I won't allow you, or my stupid ass ex-husband to control me. This..." she waved her hands between us, "...was a mistake."

Okay, so this wasn't about me at all.

But I didn't like being lumped in with that bitch ass nigga that was her husband.

"Don't compare me to none of these fucking lames, Melanie. I'm not them."

"You want to control me. What's the difference?"

"I want your pleasure, your respect, and your trust."

"And what do I get in return? Another fucking broken heart?"

I rubbed my beard in exasperation. This shit was going left quick.

What the fuck happened with her ex?"

I knew none of this shit wasn't about me, but whatever was going on was having her second guess our situation.

"Have I given you any reason to doubt me, Melanie? No. Not one. I'm here checking on you because I was worried about you, and I missed your ass. You know how many times I've done some shit like that? ZERO!"

"Oh, so I should feel special that you don't just want to tie me up and lock me in your sex dungeon?"

I looked around to make sure Naomi wasn't anywhere in sight before moving closer to Melanie and gripping her firmly by the neck.

I saw her chest rise, and her lips part.

I knew she wasn't unaffected.

Shit, the closeness to her had my body aching for her.

"Don't do that. Don't disrespect me, Melanie. I'm here trying to give you more than anything I've ever given to another individual, in my entire life. Don't put me in some box with these other worthless muthafuckas."

"I didn't ask you for more. I remember you specifically telling me that you didn't have more to give. Keep that same energy."

I was truly befuddled.

Her ex-husband must have done something crazy.

But I wasn't about to be her punching bag. So, I let go of her and took a step back.

As soon as there was space between us, I instantly missed her energy.

However, her mouth, her attitude was more than I had ever allowed a submissive to direct my way.

So, I was backing the hell off.

And this is exactly why I don't do shit outside of my set perimeters. I never fucking learn!

I stuffed my hands in my pockets, and stared at Melanie.

"You sure you want me to leave?"

Melanie couldn't make eye contact with me. She looked to the ground, and I wanted to go back to her to pick her chin up. But I held firm in my position. I needed her to make this decision on my own, because I could see she was warring with some shit.

"Tennessee."

It was low, a tiny whisper, but I heard her.

The word leaving her lips was like a blow to the gut.

I never wanted her to have to use it, but here we were.

Melanie couldn't even pick her head up to look me in the eye. And like the true Dom I was, I was going to honor that safe word.

I turned to leave, without saying another damn word.

I was beyond vexed that I was ready to tell her that I wanted her in every way, for her to fucking treat me like shit over some shit that absolutely had nothing to do with me.

Chapter Twenty-Nine

MELANIE

I was so fucked up over Gordon trying me. Over Warrick walking out on me, and over not being able to control my emotions.

I went from being on a high to downright depressed.

I was currently sitting at the kitchen island with Sinaa, drinking away my woes.

I had to fly to Clarington in three days, and I didn't want to think about the possibilities of that shit. I definitely didn't want to think about Warrick walking out of my condo, and not even attempting to get in contact with me again.

It was my fault, I know. But still... I wanted him to try a little harder.

He was there telling me he basically had deeper feelings for me, and I stood there, with a brave face, putting him back in the box he created for us.

Was that the right thing?

"Mel, slow the hell down," Sinaa said as she took the bottle of tequila from my hand.

"What? I'm safe. I don't plan on driving. I just wanna drink."

"Why are you letting Gordon get you this worked up? You know he's not going to win this battle, right?"

Oh, if only she knew.

I didn't tell her what happened between Warrick and I because I didn't want her to get worried and go running her mouth to my LITTLE brother.

I grumbled, and snatched the bottle back.

After three more shots, I started bawling.

"Girl, what the fuck is wrong with you? I know you are not this emotional over some damn court case. Did something else happen?" She paused. "Shit. Did something happen between you and Warrick?"

I grumbled again, and this time I didn't even bother with the shot glass. I just took the bottle to the head.

"O.M.G.−something did happen, didn't it?"

"Did he hurt you?"

I looked at her crazy over the bottle.

"Why the fuck would you ask that?"

"Well, Malachi told me he's into BDSM, like hardcore."

See... pillow talking.

"He did not hurt me, Sinaa."

Before I could even elaborate further, Malachi stormed into the damn kitchen with a look of rage on his face.

"What's wrong, babe?" Sinaa asked him.

Malachi stormed right past his wife and over to me, snatching the body out of my hands.

"This nigga gripped you up by the throat?"

Sinaa's eyes went wide.

"Mel, I thought you said he didn't hurt you?"

"He didn't. Malachi, what are you talking about?"

"I was standing outside of Zinae's room, and Naomi was telling her that he stormed your condo, and gripped you up by the neck."

That little girl!

"Malachi, she doesn't know what she's talking about."

"He didn't grip you up?"

"He didn't hurt me, Malachi."

That was all the confirmation he needed.

He stormed to the front door and slammed it so damn hard.

I prayed he was just going to take a drive and let his anger simmer down, but deep in my drunken gut, I knew different.

Fuck!

Chapter Thirty

WARRICK

I was sitting behind the camera, wrapping up a segment of The War Room when all hell seems to break loose on set.

There's a lot of noise, and I try to stay focused on the teleprompter. After hearing a loud crash, I looked over with a raised brow to the camera man.

He nodded, as if telling me to continue, so I assumed that everything is good.

There's always an angry wife or girlfriend that seems to get past security and storm the set with some type of drama. And we normally keep rolling because the shit is always hilarious and provides good outtakes.

Then, I realize that everything is not fine, and that I am about to be the butt of the outtakes today.

Before I can fully register what's happening, Malachi stormed up to the desk I'm sitting behind, and punched me square in my damn jaw.

I see his ass ain't loose that speed.

My thought left me just as quickly as it came because Malachi seemed to only have gotten started in his attack. His quick steps mirrored a defender rushing the line after a snap.

"Didn't I tell you that you would have to see me if you fucking hurt my sister?"

The daze of his hit faded, and his words registered.

I started to see red.

I told him to mind his damn business, and now I was going to have to fuck him up because he didn't heed my warning.

All of this goes through my brain in what seems like slow motion, but it was really all occurring at lightning speed.

I'm quickly forced to dip the left hook Malachi tried to follow up with his jab.

On the way back up, I connect a punishing blow to his kidney.

I was sure that would have slowed him down, but Malachi recovered much quicker than a regular man, and we continued to go blow for blow.

I don't know how long we were trying to beat the shit out of one another, but security was finally able to get between us, holding Malachi back.

I threw my head to the side and spit out blood that pulled in my mouth from a busted lip.

Both Malachi and I were bruised, busted, and bleeding.

I had to give it to him; he had major heart, because he was still trying to break free from security and get to me.

I really didn't know why Malachi was rushing my ass. His sister was the one who used her gotdamn safe word and put me the fuck on ice.

I tried to change the rules, but she put my ass right in my place, gutting me with the use of her safe word.

And I wasn't feeling that shit. I tried to use our Dom-Sub relationship to get things to go my way, but again, Melanie shut that down.

I don't even know why I was letting myself lose control with this girl. Control was everything to me, but it quickly slipped through my hands as soon as I got involved with Melanie.

Melanie could pretend that she wasn't affected by the last weekend we spent together, and all the shit we'd done. I would give her space, but I knew she wanted me just as much as I wanted her.

I simply needed to figure out how we could both get what we wanted, but also maintain control and not lose myself to my past.

But shit... first I gotta figure out what the hell Melanie wants.

Melanie left me the hell confused. And I didn't like her dealing with whatever from her ex and taking it out on me.

But right now, I seriously wanted to hurt her brother for making a damn spectacle on my show. I'm sure my chances of being able to figure shit out with Melanie would be diminished after she hears about this shit.

"I'm going to fuck you up, Warrick. On sight... every time I see you, muthafucka! You made a mistake putting your fucking hands on my sister." Malachi was yelling and still struggling against the security's hold.

"I'm not going to tell you again, Malachi. Mind your damn business. I don't know what the fuck you heard, but I didn't put my hands on Melanie, in that way."

"Yeah, okay, nigga!"

Security finally forced Malachi out of the studio, still spewing his threats.

I wiped at my lip, spit out some more blood, and headed for my dressing room.

"Arghh!"

I yelled out into the empty room.

I knew I should have stayed the hell away from Melanie.

I knew I shouldn't have had a taste of her.

Because I couldn't let her go. But as much as I wanted her, I didn't think I could do a typical relationship. I couldn't do the husband/wife shit.

I didn't know how to be a damn husband.

However, there were feelings swirling in my gut that I couldn't get rid of. I was the one who was starting to want *more,* while Melanie somehow was managing to stay true to the outline of our situation.

Maybe she wasn't, and that's why Malachi was trying to beat my ass, I thought.

Maybe she wasn't handling the break in what had become our normal routine.

And I definitely wanted to know why Malachi thought I fucking put hands on Melanie.

I would never.

I needed to see her, but I also knew I needed to step to her correct. She deserved a man to love and cherish her. And I needed to be sure that was some shit I could do.

But I was a Dom and I needed a Sub.

Even though I wanted things to go deeper with Melanie, I still needed control, and I don't know how much of a *typical* relationship would work without me feeling like I was losing control.

I needed that control. It's what saved my life.

Everything that I've ever taken control of never caused me harm.

However, every time I gave someone else power, a piece of me... it always backfired.

Always.

This has been my life as far back as I could remember. People around me always wanted to take, take, and take some more.

First it was my parents. Taking their mental illness out on me in the form of physical, and painful abuse. Then, when I was taken from them and placed with my grandparents, it was the same shit, just a different house, and a different type of abuse.

But it was always pain that I receive. So much damn pain. Never love.

I didn't even think people were truly capable of that shit.

I didn't think I was.

Melanie had me feeling real different. But I also couldn't just forget the pain I've endured throughout my life.

As soon as I decided that no one could control my mental, no matter what they did to my body, I controlled the pain. Life went my way... even if it was only in my head.

Outside of my parents, Mea and Mya's mom had me etching my control in stone after poking holes in the condom to trap me.

Then came Melanie, causing a part of me to want to give something that I didn't even know dwelled inside of me.

I introduced her to my world, and she adapted well. But this hiccup with whatever she was going through... me telling her I wanted more... trying to force my dominance over her... I fucked up.

Fucking dummy.

I should have just let her be. I should have given her the space she clearly needed.

However, my ass had to go and insert myself in her space. I wanted her to feel what I already knew deep down.

She was mine.

Initially, my mind only allowed my claim to stay within the parameters of a Dom/Sub relationship. However, I wanted everything about her to be mine, outside of whatever scene I conjured up for us.

She fucking stole my heart. My heart. It would seem as if she'd done it in the last weekend we were together, but if I had to be honest with myself, she did that shit way before.

She challenged me from our very first interaction, and I loved that shit.

Thoughts of Melanie being with anyone else, made my skin prickle and my blood to boil.

Even thoughts of her fucking lame ass ex-husband made me see red. Because he obviously did something to her to try and dim her beautiful light.

I wasn't about to let that shit happen.

She was mine. And I wanted her to know it.

For a moment, when I had her in my grasp—with the way she looked up at me—I thought she was going to say she felt the same.

But she surprised the hell out of me.

Her quick tongue washed away the satisfied, sexual haze that started to creep over my body.

Again, I was thinking about her actually using that damn safe word.

I was stunned.

Normally it was women asking for a deeper connection and me shutting them down.

This entire situation was foreign to me.

I lived by never allowing myself to open up and getting burned, but here I was, on fire from rejection because I wanted to change the terms.

I guess Melanie felt like I applied too much pressure to our situation, because it didn't seem like it was that hard for her to push me away.

Even if I wanted to fight for her, at that moment, I couldn't. As her Dom, I had to abide by our agreement. And that agreement was that I backed off immediately after she used her safe word.

I really didn't even know what to say to try to sway Melanie. My head was too fucked up. And she was too perfect and didn't deserve empty promises from anyone, especially my damaged ass.

"Fuck! FUCK! SHIT!"

Finally getting out of my head, coming back to the here and now, I punched the wall repeatedly.

The crazy thing was, I feared giving Melanie a piece of me because it would cause me to lose my tight control, but here I was, spiraling fast and hard anyways.

I felt helpless. And I didn't like that.

The last time I've had feelings of helplessness was when my grandma would take money from her friends and allow them to have sex with me.

Those thoughts took all the strength from my knees.

I slumped and slid down the wall, with tears threatening.

Yeah, my big ass was about to cry.

That's what those thoughts did to me. When I allowed my

mind to wander to the worst time in my life, my control would try and slip through my fingers.

I hadn't thought about the sexual abuse I endured from the age of eleven to sixteen in a long fucking time.

My control always kept those vile memories at bay.

I had to squeeze my eyes tight and talk myself into not going down memory lane.

But it was too late.

Thoughts of their hands, mouths, and other geriatric ass body parts on me had bile rising in my throat.

I had to reach for the nearby trash can to keep from spilling the contents of my stomach on the floor of my dressing room.

Then, I was reminded of the fact that I was in my dressing room having a mental breakdown. Mentally flipping through the last time I was with Melanie, and disturbing thoughts of my past.

There were three loud knocks on my door, and my producer stormed in.

"Damn, War, you good? Malachi kicked your ass that bad?"

"Kenneth, get the fuck out!"

Even though I told my producer to leave, I was thankful for the interruption of my thoughts.

"I just wanted to come in and tell you that ya ass is trending. I tried to get the cameraman to stop rolling, but he ignored my orders."

Yeah, right! I thought.

He's probably the one who gave the direction to not alarm me to what was coming.

Chapter Thirty-One

MELANIE

I cannot believe this shit.

My life seemed to be going so damn good. I got rid of the dead weight of Gordon's ass, relocated, got a new job, and was finding peace.

But all that shit seemed too much like right.

It had to be because I went and added dick to the equation.

Men always complicated shit.

And right now, my life went from easy breezy to very fucking complicated.

I knew when Malachi stormed out of the house, he was going to do some fuck shit. But my ass was too drunk to really compute or even stop him.

Sinaa was too in shock, because she had never really seen my brother's rage reach the level it had that day, so she also let him storm out of the house.

Now, I was the new breaking story all across social media,

and not to mention ESPN since Warrick was a retired football player, who was still very relevant.

First, it was the damn fight between him and Malachi breaking the damn internet. Then the blogs had to go and do their *research,* and put their own spin on shit, finding out about my identity in the process.

The media, especially here in Miami, already suspected how Warrick got down in his private time, even with all the exclusivity he claimed he had come with his acquired tastes.

But in today's society, nothing was ever really a secret. There was always someone willing and ready to run their damn mouth for the right price, no matter if it were the truth, or who it could potentially hurt.

I don't even know where the hell the grainy images of Warrick and I out and about on the few dates we did go on came from. But these blogs had the damn patience of a gnat. They had to be annoying as hell, to have scoured whatever resources to find that shit.

I'm just glad that Warrick never actually took me to his exclusive club, because they even had a little bit of information on that shit.

I would have died inside if I were connected to a sex club. Truth be told, I was already dying inside, being stamped as a submissive.

That shit was a little embarrassing. My damn daughter and niece, as heavy as they are on social media, found all of this shit immediately.

I felt their stares and heard their whispers.

Trying to be an adult, I put all of it out of my mind because I had lessons to plan and kids to teach. But it felt like the teachers, and even the students, knew about my scandal. I might as well have been walking around with a big ass *A* sewn into my garments, better yet, tattooed on my damn forehead.

Then to top all that shit off, I still had to go back to Clarington for this damn Contempt Hearing.

I was exhausted.

And my damn heart hurt, because I missed Warrick.

I miss the way he took control and calmed me. I miss allowing him to bring me so much pleasure that I thought of nothing but him.

The thought of how he showed up at my condo, all concerned–now I can see that he truly cared. But that day, I couldn't see past my anger. Gordon successfully fucked everything up in my head.

My emotions had me not trusting myself.

I couldn't see the forest through the trees, and I allowed Gordon's tackiness to spill over into my shit with Warrick. And I was wrong.

However, I couldn't muster up the courage to call him and tell him I was wrong.

But my body was yearning for release–yearning for him.

It was crazy how I literally put a halt to everything with just one word, but my mind was still under the influence of Warrick's dominance.

I had yet to please myself.

The thought actually made my pussy dry.

I needed his touch. His rough, yet soft, hands. And I needed his mouth. I wanted to feel the coarseness of his beard scratching the inside of my thigh as he licked and teased me with his tongue.

But again, I was too much of a punk to make the first move.

"Hey, mama. You okay?"

Naomi came and plopped down on the bed next to me and burrowed herself under my covers. I could tell she had been wary about all that was happening. She pretty much refused to leave my side, not even to spend time with her sister or her little boyfriend.

My heart swelled at the concern she'd shown for me. But I already felt like she had to grow up too fast, so I didn't want her to feel as if she needed to keep a close eye on me as if I were in the psych ward.

"I'm okay, little nugget," I told her as I ruffled her hair.

"Mama! Do you know how long it takes to get these girls to pop off? Don't touch my hair." She sang the last sentence in her best rendition of Solange's voice.

I couldn't help but laugh. Naomi was too much.

"I'm worried about you, mama. And I'm sorry that Uncle Malachi overheard me telling Zinae what I saw between you and Mr. Warrick. I know now you like that kinky stuff."

I choked on my saliva and smacked Naomi on the damn head.

"Little girl!"

She tried to hide her head under the covers, but she couldn't hold back her laugh.

"What? I saw the stories, mama. And I did some research… you're nasty!"

See… too damn grown.

"But seriously, mom. I have never seen you this down. Not even when daddy would do his dirt. I'm worried about you. Maybe you should talk to Mr. Warrick."

"Stay out of grown folks' business, Naomi."

"Yes, ma'am."

I scolded her, but it was truly heartwarming to know she cared this much. Naomi may have been a teenager, who started feeling herself lately, but she was a genuine sweetheart, and she loved me to the ends of the earth. I was thankful to have her as my daughter.

Changing the subject, Naomi told me what she had planned for the upcoming hearing with her father.

"Mama, I don't want to go to the hearing. I don't want the judge to force me to spend time with daddy. I'm just really mad at him right now. But I did write a very long letter to the judge. You can give it to Ms. Vanessa to use as an exhibit or something."

"Look at you, *use as an exhibit*. What you know about legal terminology?"

"I'm going to be an entertainment lawyer. And I'm going to represent Zinae in all her talents that I know she's going to blow up for. Ma, she's so smart! She's pushing me to want to do and be better. She choreographs for Disney, she takes amazing photos, and her YouTube content on all the black-owned brands she uses is amazing. She's going to need someone to have her back in the industry. I just hope I can make her proud and actually become a lawyer."

"Naomi, you can do anything you want. You is smart, you is kind..."

"Really, mama!" Naomi cut me off. "You're going to quote *The Help?*"

I shrugged.

"What? You quoted Solange."

"You're so lame."

"You love me, though. And thank you for wanting to tell your side of the story for this hearing. I really appreciate you having my back. And I'm also sorry for you even having to be in this position."

"You're my world, mama."

"And you're mine."

"But I'ma need you to go get your man back. I'ont like all of this time you have to keep your attention on me."

"That's because you want to sneak off and go fool around with that little boy. You ain't slick."

"I think I love him, mama."

I rolled my damn eyes.

"You're sixteen, Naomi. No need to rush. There are going to be plenty of Romans in your life."

"I don't know, ma. Roman is everything..."

Naomi trailed off, and I watched the starry-eyed expression settle into her face.

I'm screwed!

"Don't let that boy and his little penis have you distracted from your plans. You just said you wanted to be an entertainment attorney. Focus on that."

"Mom, can you not talk about his junk?"

"What? I know y'all are having sex. I wish you wouldn't, but I can't be with you every minute of every day. But I'm telling you... stay focused, Naomi."

"I will. I promise."

I trusted my daughter to make smart decisions, so I just hoped she wouldn't lose herself to a boy, and end up down the wrong path.

"I believe you."

"Now, are you going to call Mr. Warrick?"

"Didn't I tell your ass to stay out of grown folks' business? I can be in yours; you can't be in mine. Now get out. I'm going to bed."

Naomi rolled her eyes, but climbed out of my bed and headed for the door.

I looked over at my phone charging on the nightstand, and thought about picking it up to call Warrick. But something just stopped me.

Maybe after this hearing, I tried to convince myself.

———

I met Vanessa across the street from the courthouse, with big shades on, and dressed to kill. I wasn't about to stroll up in that hearing looking like how I felt. Which was a downright depressed, sexually frustrated mess.

It was funny how I hadn't let Gordon's ass touch me in years, and I was completely fine without having sex. But after a few months in Warrick's care, my body craved the feeling of intimacy like it never has, and I was going through major withdrawal.

However, I had to stay firm. Warrick wanted a submissive, and while I could give him that in the bedroom, I wasn't quite sure if I could outside of the bedroom. And I didn't want to believe his proclamation of wanting more, giving in, and not being enough for him.

"Hey, Mel. How are you feeling?"

I was forced to put my thoughts of Warrick aside. I needed to anyway because I had started obsessing.

"Hey, Vanessa. I'm just ready for this day to be over with. And I hope that Gordon will just crawl under a damn rock for the next two years after this."

Vanessa chuckled.

"That's not likely, but I'll see what magic I can work today. We'll worry about tomorrow when it comes."

"I guess. Let's head over."

We walked out of the coffee shop and over to the courthouse.

My case was called immediately and we got situated up front in front of the judge's bench.

I had to do a double-take while Vanessa was unpacking her things.

Seated behind me was Malachi.

I glared at him. I hadn't talked to him since he blew up my damn life with that damn fight video. That shit was still making its rounds. So much so, the damn principal at the school suggested I take a fucking leave of absence.

Malachi stared back at me unmoved by the murderous glare I was giving him. He actually looked to be taunting me—daring me to say something to him.

I didn't, but I was going to curse his ass out after this damn hearing.

I was also going to kick Sinaa's ass for not telling me he planned on coming today. But I guess it was my own fault, because I had been blocking everyone out lately.

"All rise. Calling the case of Brown vs. Brown."

The bailiff pulled me out of my thoughts.

And I had to control my eye roll at the mention of the case caption. I hated still being referred to as Brown. But I understood that's what the case was initially filed under. I just couldn't wait for this to be over and the entire case was closed.

"You may be seated. Are all parties present?" The judge addressed the courtroom.

"Vanessa Spelling, Your Honor, counsel for Melanie Long, formally Melanie Brown."

"Sheldon Namen, counsel for Gordon Brown."

"Glad to see your client is on time today, Mr. Namen."

I smiled.

That was a good sign. The judge remembered Gordon's fuck up from before and apparently knew how to hold a grudge.

The hearing started, and Gordon and his attorney jumped out the gate with a bunch of dumbass accusations.

And of course, Gordon went for the jugular and tried to use my recent appearance in the blogs as a way to make me look like a bad mother.

"Your Honor, not only is Ms. Long keeping my client's child from him, she's also relocated his child and has been in less than stellar situations. Ms. Long has been recently featured in blogs for less than unsavory things. I will use discretion and not mention them on the record, but I will request to enter exhibits detailing these allegations."

"Objection. As already proved by my exhibits, Mr. Brown has refused to make arrangements for getting his child, actually canceling on her. After several canceled visits, their child, who is sixteen, refused to participate in being let down repeatedly. Ms. Long feels as though a sixteen-year-old can make an emotional decision to not want to be constantly let down. Thus, this direction in which Mr. Namen is trying to take this hearing is irrelevant. He is simply trying to bring in issues that were out of my client's control, to simply embarrass her."

I was holding my damn breath. Because the entire shit with Warrick and Malachi fighting, leading me to be outed as Warrick's new sub was mortifying.

"I'd like to look at these exhibits before determining if I will allow them to be entered."

I held my breath the entire time the judge reviewed the documents. Some of those blog stories were terrible, ragging on my non-traditional Miami girl appearance, shading the fact that I was a schoolteacher, and even calling me a gold digger who was cut off by her brother, looking for her next checks.

The shit was just mean.

I looked over at Vanessa for some support.

She smiled back at me, but I could tell she had no idea which way this was going to go.

Finally, the judge looked up at me over her readers. I could not make out her expression. I wanted to cover my face from shame, but I remained solid in my stature and kept eye contact.

"Objection sustained."

The breath that left my chest felt like I was being let up after a sumo wrestler had me pinned down.

"Is there anything else that the parties would like to submit into evidence?"

"Your Honor, I have a letter from the parties' sixteen-year-old daughter, Naomi Brown."

"Objection. She's a minor."

"She is sixteen, a bright student, and has thrived in Ms. Long's care long before the couples even split. What she has to say is important. How she feels is important."

"Your client could have told her to write whatever is in that letter. How do we know that she wasn't coerced into writing things that make my client look bad?"

The gavel banged, causing me to jump.

"Enough!"

"I will read the letter, and then I will determine if it has any weight on my decision."

Because this was contempt hearing, it went by quick. Funny thing, Gordon's ass wasn't even really asking that he get time with Naomi. He was more focused on me paying his outlandish attorney fees.

The judge didn't even break. She looked over everything right there before us.

"Mr. Gordon... you have a very smart young daughter. And she loves you. It's apparent in this letter, but you have let her down a number of times. I would suggest you really try to get things right before it's too late."

Gordon hung his head at the judge's words. He actually looked ashamed.

"Ms. Long, I am not going to hold you in contempt. You have proven that you have tried to foster a relationship between your daughter and Mr. Brown. However, I am going to order that the two of them do some type of unification therapy. I will allow it to be virtual as you no longer live in Tennessee. Mr. Gordon, if you miss another visitation with your daughter, and Ms. Long allows for her to make the decision to spend time with you on her own, please do not file anything in my courtroom. I don't want to see any more frivolous filing come across my desk for this matter. You understand?"

"Yes, Your Honor."

"I am ordering reunification therapy, and denying both parties' petition for attorney fees."

The gavel was banged, and court was dismissed.

I didn't win, but I didn't exactly lose either.

I was just hoping that this was the last time I would have to deal with any legal issues with this fool.

I strolled out of the courtroom, ignoring Gordon, and my damn brother.

But it would have been too much like right for everything to go on without any drama.

"I fucking hate you. You're so pathetic that you had to go and be someone's sex slave. Nasty hoe."

Of course, it was Gordon behind me spewing his shit. But I long ago stopped caring what the hell he thought.

I just shook my head and wondered why the hell did I ever think being with him was a good idea.

Ick!

I was absolutely disgusted with myself.

"Nigga, didn't I tell you not to utter another fucking word in my sister's direction? I know I fucking told you I would beat the shit out of you."

Got dammit!

Here came Malachi trying to come to my fucking rescue... again.

"Malachi! Calm the fuck down. Just let it go. He's not worth it."

Instead of listening, Malachi continued in his pursuit of Gordon. I had to just get between them before he did something stupid.

"Malachi! Are you really getting ready to fucking get into a fight outside of the damn courthouse? So, they can lock your ass up? I'm going to fucking leave you there."

Malachi was furious, but he didn't advance further.

"Gordon, please just go. Please," I said to him when I turned to face him. "I don't know why you have these deep feelings of hatred for me, but please... let me be... you're the one who caused us to come to an end. If you never do anything else for me, can you just please let me be?"

Maybe it was the plea in my voice, or the desperation in my tone, or the tears that was threatening to slip from my eyes, because Gordon turned and walked away without a word.

I breathed deep, thankful for this once grace.

Then I turned to my brother, with rage lighting my eyes.

"Malachi! MIND YOUR FUCKING BUSINESS!" I yelled at him.

A few heads turned our way, but I didn't give a damn.

"I'm just trying to protect you, sis."

My anger only flared.

"I am almost forty fucking years old. I don't need you protecting me. I'm good. I got it. Unless I come to you and ask for your help, stay the fuck out of my life. You were just about to make another fucking scene over me. What happens when that goes viral, huh? Now the blogs really will feel the need to dig into my life. Don't you think you fucking did enough?"

Malachi stuffed his hands in his pockets and looked away.

"You weren't thinking of me at all. You were thinking of you, Malachi. Because if you were thinking of me, in either situation, you would have known that I hate drama. That I hate being the center of attention. That I don't like causing friction."

I knew my brother's intentions were pure, but he wasn't thinking shit through, and it was affecting my life. I couldn't let that shit slide.

"Where you going, Mel?"

"To the fucking airport to get out of this damn town. And away from you!"

I was so glad he didn't follow, because I didn't want to have

to step outside of my character and have to beat my baby brother's ass.

I needed silence, and alone time.

I needed Warrick. And I wanted to cry over the way I
pushed him away.

The fact that I used my safe word.

I saw that it gutted him. He was opening up to me, and I
shut him down.

On the entire way out of this shitty town, I tried to talk
myself into calling him, but I still couldn't.

I was scared.

Chapter Thirty-Two

WARRICK

I was really laying low lately. The media was having a damn field day with the fight I had with Malachi. I hadn't seen my face on T.V. this much—outside of my show—in years. Wasn't nobody really checking for a retired football player, turned T.V. personality.

But here I was damn near ten years post-NFL days, making my way around the damn blogs.

I was so thankful that my phone numbers were private, because I could barely take all the weird ass emails that came into my work email.

Black Twitter was so intrigued about me being into BDSM. I guess it ain't enough of us out here in the world, so I have been offered so much damn money to do all kinds of interviews, even been offered a hundred grand to do an interview/demonstration. I ain't have no damn idea what that consisted of, but I was good as hell.

I only operated under major discretion. If Malachi ain't come and make a damn scene, none of this shit would be happening.

I couldn't stop thinking about Melanie, though.

I knew all of this had to be tough on her. Doing something I never did, I looked her up on social media to see if she was posting anything, but I didn't find anything.

I just wanted her to be okay. But I wouldn't reach out. She used her safe word.

Melanie would have to come to me.

At least I hoped I could hold out long enough not to break my own rule.

My phone buzzed on my desk, breaking me out of my musings.

"Hello?"

"Is this Warrick Jones?"

Damn, someone got my number.

"Who is this, and how can I help you? I am a very busy man, so if this isn't important, please do not waste my time."

"My name is Patrice. I'm calling from Horizon Medical Center. Your grandmother has been here for cancer treatment for the past three months. She's very lucky and will be able to go home soon, Mr. Jones. She also instructed us to reach out to you regarding her medical bills."

My mind was fucking blown.

Why the fuck would Wilamina Jones think I would ever give a fuck about her, her cancer, or her bills?

That bitch made me a sex slave for five damn years.

She sold me to the highest bidders amongst her friends. In the beginning, she would monitor me, making sure I was *performing.* My grandmother was pure fucking evil.

I had to breathe deep, because I didn't want to be taken to

that place. This was already the second time in recent weeks that I've thought about something that I was sure I put out of mind.

I didn't even bother with asking the woman's name on this line.

"Ma'am, you can tell my grandmother that I hope her death is long, slow, and torturous, and when she finally goes, that she burns in hell with gasoline drawers on."

Then I fucking hung up the phone.

I needed release. I needed to get my control back in place, but there was nothing that could help me with that at the moment.

But when I finally got control of my emotions, what shocked me the most wasn't that I needed to have controlled sex; what I needed was to hold Melanie. She calmed me. Her purity did more for me than any scene could do.

I know I told myself that I was going to let her come to me, but I didn't think I was going to make it if she didn't reach out soon.

Because what I thought was a pretty solid life, was quickly shaping up to be held together by band-aids. With Melanie though, I felt like my wounds were exposed, but she alone was healing them without even knowing.

She didn't know half of what I'd gone through in life. I already saw that she was holding in her pity when I told her I was abused. I didn't want her to look at me like that. I wanted to remain strong—dominant—in her eyes.

Now though, I feel like Melanie was the only person who could get me together.

Melanie, I need you, baby.

That wasn't actually as hard to admit as I thought it would

be. I've never needed anyone once I ran away at sixteen, and I promised myself that I would never rely on anyone. But here I was, needing Melanie like I needed air to breathe. The shit was a realization that shocked me to my core, but not quite in a bad way.

Admitting that to myself, had me feeling lighter already.

Now, I just need you to come back to me, Mel.

Just as I was ready to give in, my doorbell rang.

I was hoping that Melanie heard my calls for her, and she had come to mend my soul.

Soon as I headed down the steps and saw who was standing on the other side of my damn glass door, I was annoyed.

Making it to the foyer, I swung the door open.

"What the fuck are you doing here, Malachi? I thought I told you to mind your fucking business."

"Yeah, you and my sister."

"Bruh, I really need you to back off then."

I didn't even have the rah-rah energy in me. The call about my grandmother, the way my mind and body craved Melanie... I just didn't have a right in me.

"Listen, I came here to apologize."

That took me by surprise. Especially if he thought I put my hands on Melanie.

The start of this apology had me curious, so I opened the door wider and moved to the side, allowing Malachi in.

When we reached the kitchen, I grabbed two beers out of the fridge, and handed him one. I wanted to be pissed, but I couldn't even manage the emotion. Because if I had a sister, I'm sure I would have done anything in my power to protect her.

"Listen, War... I don't like this shit between you and Melanie..."

"That don't sound like an apology, nigga," I interrupted.

"Man, will you shut the fuck up and let me finish. Damn. Like I was saying, I can't say that any brother would be feeling her fucking around with the shit you're into. I already don't want to think about my sister's personal life on that level, but to then have to block out thoughts that she liked being tied and beat and shit... it's a lot for me. But I was wrong for that shit I did, with coming to your job. Deep down, I knew you wouldn't hurt Melanie, but the thought of you putting your hands on her that way in front of my niece... I just snapped."

"Khi, you know I would never do no shit like that. I didn't know Naomi was eavesdropping, and it wasn't nothing like that, yo."

Malachi rubbed his hands down his face. We were cool as shit, but I could see that he was still somewhat at an impasse, because he still couldn't fully accept what his sister and I had going on.

"Melanie means more to me than anyone. I have never felt this way about someone."

"I know. I know ya ass was holding back when I came for you. And I know it was only on the strength of Melanie. I woulda kicked your ass either way, but I could tell you ain't wanna fight me."

"Bruh, you can't take me. You better be lucky I fucking love ya sister. Otherwise, I would have had to flatline ya ass."

Silence filled the room.

I thought I was funny... I was just joking, but Malachi's ass was staring me down like he wanted a repeat of what happened in the studio.

He finally spoke.

"You really love my sister?"

Shit, I didn't even realize I said that shit out loud. I have been thinking it for a minute, but for it to actually slip from between my lips shocked me just as much as it was shocking Malachi. But it was out there now. I couldn't take it back. Didn't want to take it back.

"Yeah, man."

"You too old for her," is what Malachi responded with.

I chuckled, " Nigga, I'm only four years older than Mel."

"Man, I need to find something to stick, besides the obvious."

I chuckled.

"Thanks for coming here, Khi. I appreciate it."

"I'm doing this for Melanie. After my fight with you, then almost beating her ex-husband's ass, she's pretty much threatened to kick me out of her life. This is the longest we have gone with talking to one another. I want my sister back, and if that means ignoring this shit... then I gotta do what I gotta do."

"Malachi, you know I'd never hurt Melanie, right?"

"Man, deep down, I know that shit. I know you're a good dude, Warrick. You just have a fucked-up past."

"True, but I would protect Melanie with my life."

"I hear you. You can go and protect her right now, because I am assuming that Mel has stressed herself out so much that she's made herself physically sick. She has the flu, and she won't let me in to help."

I got up from my seat.

"That was all you needed to say. All that other shit wasn't necessary. My lady is sick, and you wanna run your mouth."

"Mannn... I can see it now; you're going to be a pain in my ass."

I clapped Malachi on the back as we headed for the door.

"But I got your sister, though. You the one who let her end up with a bum all those years ago."

"Man, I hate that I wasn't old enough to stop that shit."

I chuckled, because even if he was, Melanie would have told him the same thing back then, *to mind his fucking business.*

"We good, Khi?" I asked, closing the door behind us

"We good. As long as you take care of Melanie. I don't have any issues."

"Then we're good."

I watched Malachi hop in his truck, and I hopped in mine, heading out right behind him.

This was the sign I needed.

I was going to go get my lady, and for the first time in my life, cross lines that I've never even thought about crossing.

Shit. You already crossed them. Your dumbass is just finally acknowledging it.

I couldn't even disagree with my inner thoughts.

I didn't care to think on it any further. Melanie in my arms was my only mission.

Chapter Thirty-Three

MELANIE

In the past month I survived being a submissive, getting sued by ex-husband, witnessed my brother and my–I guess Dom–fight spread through social media like wildfire, get thrown as fuel to said fire, being described as Warrick's new plaything, and get forced to take a leave of absence from work.

My life had become a damn circus. And I was over it.

And now... I was suffering with the damn flu.

I thought I was a good human being. I thought I put forth good efforts to help the less fortunate, read my Bible, and I prayed. Shit I even recycled, dammit!

Why was Karma doing this to me? I ain't do shit to that vindictive heaux!

I wanted to cry. But I was so damn dehydrated that not even a half of an actual tear would actually fall from my lids. And now someone was on the other side of my door, making me have to move my achy bones.

"Warrick, what are you doing here?"

It took all of the energy I had to get to the door. And I wish I would have just ignored it.

I was kicking myself for sending Naomi with Malachi and Sinaa. She would have come in handy right about now. But I really didn't want to spread my germs, then the next thing she had the flu. Also, if I were forced to deal with Warrick, I definitely didn't want Naomi's ass around for that. Malachi and Warrick be done started World War III with her recap of what she thinks is going on with Warrick and I.

Using all my energy to get to the door, to see Warrick on the other, drained me emotionally, in addition to the physical depletion I felt.

I wanted to immediately close the door in his face, because looking at him hurt. I missed him like hell. I have yearned for him every day that I didn't have his touch.

However, seeing his tall, broad frame towering over me, had my body awakening and my mind more lucid than it had been in days. It was as if his presence instinctually woke the submissive I knew he'd come to like so much.

And I had come to love him.

But I couldn't fully allow myself to give into him.

I saw the torment behind his eyes, and it was as if I were a seer, getting a glimpse of the future... I knew Warrick could hurt me. And while the sex was out of this world, I would not subject myself to another man, who didn't have his shit together.

I knew Warrick was nothing like Gordon. However, that didn't mean he couldn't hurt me any less. I felt like he could hurt me more actually. The feelings that had quickly grown for him told me he could hurt me far worse than Gordon's sorry ass. I allowed Warrick not only into my body, but into my soul.

His touch—his energy—everything about him called to me.

It was as if I were a true submissive at the mercy of her Dom.

It scared the ever-loving shit out of me.

However, as long as we were both keeping up the facade of a simple physical relationship, I felt like my heart was okay to play along.

The moment he began to express a deeper connection to me, my flight instincts kicked all the way in. Especially right after the mess Gordon continued to try to put me through.

Our shit was already too intense. I couldn't imagine the power he would wield over me if I gave all of me to him.

That shit I just couldn't do.

I had to preserve myself.

I knew I was lying through my teeth as the thoughts crossed my mind. I knew I would end up giving all of myself to Warrick, and only prayed that he didn't break me.

Staring up at him, I couldn't deny how much I missed his ass.

And I was currently too weak physically to put up much of a fight.

"Can I come in?" He asked, breaking through my thoughts.

"I guess," I said and rolled my eyes. I had to keep my tough exterior in place, or else Warrick was bound to take control over all of me—mind, body, and spirit.

Truth be told, he already had all of that, but I wouldn't let him in on that detail.

But the way he smiled at me and walked through my condo as if he belonged, his ass already knew that shit.

I appreciated the appearance he kept up, though. Allowing me to feel like I had some control over the situation when I knew I absolutely had none.

The only power I felt in our current situation was keeping the pussy from him. But he probably didn't care about that shit... I'm sure he had bitches lined up to fulfill his needs.

Thoughts of Warrick with other women, helped me keep up the facade of being unfazed by him.

"I heard you were sick. I bought you some medicine and some soup. You have to stay hydrated."

I looked at Warrick like he was the hell crazy.

How the hell did he know I was sick?

I had to ask myself that question, because I know Malachi's ass didn't tell him.

That video of them fighting was embarrassing as hell. And between that and the shit at the courthouse, I wasn't talking to my brother. He probably only knew I was sick because of either his loudmouth niece or wife.

A part of me wanted to climb back in Warrick's bed - or sex dungeon - just to piss my brother off. Malachi walked around so damn happy, and assumed no one was experiencing his level of happiness.

While Warrick and I weren't headed for marital bliss, I was happy before things went sideways. Before he tried to take ownership of me outside of a sexual nature.

"How did you know I was sick?"

Warrick smirked at me from the kitchen, as he unloaded the contents in his bag.

"I don't know if I am allowed to tell you. That wasn't discussed, but fuck it... Malachi came by my house today."

Well shit! I was wrong as shit about my brother.

The thought brought a smile to my face—made me want to forgive his little annoying ass.

The smugness on his face annoyed me. And the way he leaned on my island made me twist my face up.

Here I was trying hard to pretend I wasn't affected by Warrick, while he was just so comfortable and relaxed–conversing with me like we haven't gone over a month without talking to one another. We were supposed to be forgetting the other even existed.

But I was lying to myself if I ever thought I would forget Warrick Jones.

There was no forgetting his sexy, domineering ass.

After messing around in my kitchen, he walked over with a serving tray topped with orange juice, chicken noodle soup, water, and a small vase with an assortment of fresh flowers.

This was definitely some shit a man would do for his woman, and I couldn't keep the smile off my face.

Let me find out he's trying to show a different side of himself.

However, when someone shows you who they are, you better believe their asses. I've already made that mistake once. I won't do it again. Because nothing about Warrick screams happily-ever-after.

But I want it so bad... and with him!

Ughhh!

I could not get a hold of myself. It had to be this flu. My immune system and brain were compromised.

"Here, try some of this." Warrick lifted my feet, sat down, then placed them gently on his lap.

"I'm not hungry, Warrick. And my throat is burning."

"Mel, you need to at least get some fluids in you. I don't want you to get dehydrated, because then I'm gonna have to take your ass to the hospital."

I rolled my eyes, and kept to myself that I really felt like I was already dehydrated.

"Why are you here, Warrick? I'm not your woman. This..." I waved my hand between us, "... is not what we do, or did. We... fuck."

"Damn, Melanie, I'm trying here."

"Did I ask you to try to do anything other than making me come?"

I watched as Warrick rubbed his hands down his face, then stroked his bread. Even my germ-ridden kitty couldn't stop from purring.

"Listen, Melanie..." I stared back at his ass because he didn't say anything following his statement. His eyes were swimming with emotion, and he looked to be warring with himself on speaking his mind. "I'm feeling things with you that I haven't ever felt. I feel like I need you. And not in a submissive way. I just need your energy near me. I'm sure it doesn't make sense to you, because it doesn't make sense to me."

Warrick let out a breath. And I kind of felt bad because I knew this was the first time he probably ever had feelings with a woman outside of his regular Dom/Sub scenarios, let alone try to express said feelings.

I knew I should have put him out of his misery and helped him along, but I was sick, and I felt like being petty.

So, my petty ass coughed and decided to take a sip of the soup he prepared for me.

Picking up on my vibe, Warrick sighed again, but this time he looked me dead in the eyes.

"Fuck, Melanie... can you stop looking at me so damn unbothered? I'm trying to tell ya ass that I'm falling the hell in love with you."

Well, hell!

I wasn't expecting that shit. I mean, I knew he liked me, but loved... that was... unexpected.

I coughed again, but it had nothing to do with my damn flu symptoms.

He jumped up and pulled me to him.

"Are you okay?"

He rubbed my back and looked down at me.

After collecting myself, I looked back up at Warrick, and I saw all the love shining in his eyes.

I didn't know what to hell to do.

Warrick had been unlike anything I had ever experienced and I figured I was just getting a little rebound dick, but here I was... in the arms of a man who claimed he was falling in love with me, and I was busy talking myself down from that ledge of love. It didn't work out for me the first time, so I didn't trust it.

But if I had to be honest, I've fallen in love with Warrick before I even understood what was taking place inside of me regarding those emotions. They were there, waiting for me to play catch up.

However, I was not about to tell his ass I loved him. I wasn't about to give him the power to play with my damn heart.

NOPE! Not today!

The way he took charge over everything in and out of the bedroom, had me ready to do and be whatever, but admit those three words.

I had to be sure that I wanted to do the things that I knew would come along with loving Warrick, because I knew there was a possibility he could railroad my ass.

Already, my mind and body couldn't get on the same page. I wanted to give Warrick the cold shoulder, but my body was slowly melting into him as he held me in his arms. Even though I stopped coughing.

We both knew he just wanted to hold me, and I allowed him.

Warrick ran his hands down the side of my face. My heart was trying to beat out of my chest and land in his hands. It wanted him... in every way.

"I can't stop it, Melanie. I tried, but damn girl, you got some voodoo essence. I can't pull away from you even if I wanted to." He leaned down and brushed his lips against mine. "Give me a chance to love you, Melanie. I can be what you need. I can step outside of my role as a Dom to be the man you need."

"But what if I want you to be my man and my Dom?"

I didn't even know where the question came from, because his needs were what held me back from allowing myself to feel these emotions for Warrick in the first place.

But the thought of just having a regular vanilla relationship turned me off.

I'd come to love how Warrick tied me up, spanked me, and all the other kinky shit he came out of left field with. I didn't ever want that to stop.

He kissed my lips again.

"Whatever you want, Melanie."

"I want you to stop kissing me because you're going to get sick. Who's going to take care of you if we both get the flu? Because my brother would happily come over here and end it all for you."

He chuckled.

"Don't worry about Malachi. He and I are good. And don't worry about me. I'll be fine. I don't get sick."

"Yeah, okay. Don't be coming over here begging for me to take care of you when you get sick."

Warrick took the bowl of soup from my hands, because I was clearly not eating it. First, I didn't have an appetite, and now my thoughts were too consumed with me and Warrick as... I didn't know what we were. But regardless, my brain wasn't firing on all cylinders.

And my eyes were starting to get droopy with all of the meds I had taken to try and beat whatever was holding my body hostage.

Before I could let sleep take me, I managed to ask what I thought was a very important question.

"So, what are we, Warrick?"

He didn't answer right away, but then I heard him say, "You're mine, Melanie. You always have been."

I couldn't say anything else. All I could do was fall into a deep slumber, with a smile on my face.

———

I woke up, and it had to be somewhere in the middle of the night because the moon beaming into my bedroom from the open curtains was on full blast, illuminating my room in the beautiful glow of night.

I stretched, still feeling achy, and my clogged nostrils was what caused me to wake up.

Once the fog cleared, I was trying to remember how I even got in my bed. I hadn't had the energy to make it to my bedroom in days. I had been parked on the couch because it was close to the kitchen.

I looked around my room and found Warrick in one of the chairs across the room.

His face was half concealed by the darkness of the room, and half was lit by the brightness of the mood flooding through the window.

It was eerie. And seemed super movie cliche. But I couldn't help the image of him surrounded by half darkness and half-light really representing who he was as a man.

I just hoped I would by sucked into the darkness.

Lord, let me be making the right decision.

"Baby, how you feeling?"

Warrick abandoned his seat and came to sit beside me on the bed.

I was glad to see he wasn't trying to climb into bed with me. At least he had some sense.

"I'm okay; my nose is just stopped up. It woke me up out of my sleep."

Warrick quickly reached for some of the meds on the bedside table and handed me a little tube for me to squirt up each nostril.

"Here, two squirts in each nostril."

I did as I was told, which I was sure he loved.

But I felt instantly better.

"Good. Now prop your head up. You need anything?"

"No, I'm good. Thank you for staying and taking care of me."

"No other place I'd rather be, Melanie. I mean that. This may be all new to me, but I feel like I want it more than I want my next breath. You bring me a peace that I have never known. Now that I've experienced it, I don't want to live without it–or you."

Damn! He was about to have my ass crying.

I tried to hold it in, but a little sniffle escaped now that my nostrils were free and clear.

"Warrick... I don't know what to say."

"You don't have to say anything. Just let me take care of you, okay?"

"Okay."

"Now, I don't normally get sick, but I'm also not invincible, so I'm going to take my ass back over to that chair."

I couldn't hold back my laugh, which turned into a cough.

"Go on, leave me to die."

Warrick chuckled, and I missed that sound so damn bad.

"Go to sleep, Melanie."

"Yes, sir!"

The air between us thickened as soon as the word left my lips.

"I... umm..."

My ass just stuttered along, because I had now damn idea what to say.

Finally, Warrick let out a chuckle.

"It's okay, baby. You said you wanted both—the man and the Dom—so you have him, baby."

"Okay."

We settled into silence again, and I was starting to doze off.

"I was raped from the ages of eleven to sixteen."

WHAT THE FUCK!

My brain could not wrap around what he just said.

Then once it did, my heart broke for him. Broke for the little boy who was violated.

"Oh my God, Warrick!"

"Shhh. Just listen."

Warrick told me all about how his parents physically abused him, then he was taken from their care and placed with his grandmother and grandfather. The rapes came after his grandmother's friends came over for a card game and told her how he was built like a grown man, and that they would pay to break him in. Warrick thought they were joking, because things seemed normal for a short while after being in their care. But it quickly turned into hell.

His grandmother took payment from her friends, then all their friends, and forced Warrick to have sex with them. And she would beat him if he underperformed. Warrick told me of all the vile things he was forced to do. And I was sick to my stomach. I wanted to get up and go to him, but he told me to stay in bed.

I could tell by the edge in his voice that he needed to control this conversation, and not being able to fully see my face was making it easier to tell his story, I'm sure.

But my heart still broke for him in the darkness.

"She apparently has cancer. I actually just got off the phone with them before Malachi came by my house and told me to come see about you. It was as if you could feel me, feel my anxiety, feel my control slipping. Because I swear, I would have never thought Khi would come to me and tell me to come see you. You don't know how that shit saved me in that moment."

"Well, I didn't tell Malachi to go to you, so I can't take the credit for that."

"I don't care how it's rationalized. I felt like your soul felt mine, and the universe was just providing an opening for you to be able to get to me."

"Again, you came to me..."

I was trying to lighten the mood, and it worked.

"Don't make me lay you over my knee and see how many smacks it takes for your Hershey ass to turn red from my palm."

Girl, don't you go jumping him. You barely have the energy to sit up.

"Warrick."

"Shh."

If he shushes me one more damn time.

You ain't gonna do shit.

Now I was having a back-and-forth conversation with myself.

I was being tormented. My attempt to change the subject and lighten the mood backfired. Now, I have a fever and not from the flu. My pussy and body were in flames for Warrick.

"Can you come lay with me? I'll turn away from you. I just need to feel you."

Warrick didn't immediately answer, but I heard him getting up. Then, as he stepped directly in the moonlit path, I could clearly make out him removing his sweatpants. I was stuck on his beauty once he was out of his t-shirt, and walking the rest of the way to the bed in just his briefs.

I couldn't even linger on the fact that this was the first time I saw Warrick dressed down, apart from when he was at the gym.

That shit was sexy, but the image of him approaching me was even better.

He walked around to the other side of the bed and climbed in, pulling my back to his front.

"There, you're getting what you want. Now go to sleep, Melanie."

"I missed you, Warrick," I told him.

He leaned over a little and whispered in my ear.

"Wait until you're better; I'm going to strap your ass to my St. Andrews Cross and have some fun."

My intake of breath was loud in the empty room. And again, I was burning up... for his touch in a nasty way. My body needed it

"Looking forward to it, sir. I haven't come since the last time we were together."

It was Warrick's turn to take in a deep breath, and I felt his dick hardening against my ass.

Point for Melanie!

"You're being a bad girl, Melanie. Go to sleep. Now."

That time I listened, and fell asleep—content in Warrick's arms.

Chapter Thirty-Four

WARRICK

"Are you going to leave me again, Melanie?" I asked as I stroked my fingers down the front of her body.

Melanie let out a whimper, but didn't answer my question.

That was a question I needed the answer to, because after pouring out my soul to her a few weeks ago while she had the flu, I didn't want to leave her damn side. But I knew I couldn't smother her that way, just because for the first time, I was doing something outside my normal perimeters.

So, the last two days, I made myself stay away from Melanie. But now, that I had her in my playroom, strapped to my St. Andrew's Cross, I was going to get all the information I wanted.

During my musings, Melanie still didn't answer my question.

"What's rule number three, Melanie? Are you going to disregard my rules?"

I slapped the front of her dripping pussy, and when I pulled my hand back, it was dripping with her essence. I brought my fingers to my lips, sniffed, and licked them clean.

"No, Sir," Melanie responded.

"No, you're not going to leave me again, or no you're not going to disregard my rules?"

I was fucking with her now, but I needed to get my point across, because she had been tempting me since I walked through the door of her apartment when she was sick. And I think this is exactly what her ass wanted.

Some of my feelings were also coming from the fact that she safe worded my ass. I couldn't believe she shut me out right after an off-the-wall weekend we had. I felt like shit when she did that, and I knew she did too, so I may have been getting a little payback in the moment.

"No, I'm not going to leave again. I need you. I love you, Sir."

At her words, I had to step back, and take in her beautiful Hershey body. I couldn't believe the words falling from her lips. It was even crazier that I believed every word of it. I was lost in her. I couldn't even form a response.

No one has ever truly needed me, or loved me, and Melanie's words almost brought me to my knees.

"You love me, Melanie?"

I was supposed to be in Dom mode. I was supposed to be punishing her. But Melanie kept fucking with my control.

"I do, baby. So much, and I'm sorry I wasn't brave enough to tell you before now."

I mentally shook my head.

The freedom Melanie just gave me somehow made me feel as light as a cloud—and heavy—at the same time.

She was telling me that I could let go of control. However, I didn't know what I would do without it.

I walked over and retrieved a box from the dresser. I hadn't intended to give this to Melanie yet, but I needed her to have it after her declaration.

I walked back to Melanie, and she held her chin high, not afraid for me to see the love in her eyes.

That only confirmed that she needed this.

I opened the box to reveal an intricately leather collar. What made it special was the breaks in the leather, which were connected by a ring of black diamonds. To the natural eye, it looked to be a simple choker necklace, but to me, it solidified our bond. If Melanie accepted my collar, she was acknowledging that she was fully giving herself to me and I would honor and protect that gift with my life.

I held it up for her to look at.

"Sir... it's beautiful," Melanie responded.

"It's my collar, Mel. It signifies that you belong to me. And if you accept this, I will put you and your wellbeing above all else. Will you take my collar, Melanie?"

She reached up and stroked her neck, and my dick bobbed with just the thought of placing the delicate piece of jewelry around her neck.

"Yes, Sir."

I let out a breath and closed the space between us, strapping the collar around her neck.

It was beautiful and laid perfectly atop her collar bone.

I stroked her face, neck, and breasts, in awe that she was giving me the treasure.

I had never collared any of my submissives. Ever. And I was thankful. Because this moment was everything. I didn't think there would ever be an end to Melanie and me, so this was worth never truly claiming another as my own.

The sexual tension between us was so damn thick.

All I could do was drop to my knees and bury my face between her plush thighs.

I knew it was only physical, but I wanted to make her feel as good as she made me feel.

"Oh, Warrick!" Melanie cried out.

I latched onto her clit and sucked her orgasm right out of her.

"Ahhhh! BABY! I'm comingggg!"

The fragrant taste of Melanie filled my mouth. It served as the perfect antidote to bring me back into my role as her Dom.

I stood to my full height and covered Melanie's mouth with mine. I made sure to keep my kiss sloppy so she could taste all of her that still lingered on my lips and tongue.

"Taste yourself, Mel. Drink all that up."

And she did.

Melanie slurped on my tongue, removing every drop of her essence from my mouth.

Once she came down from her heady high, she released the softest moan.

"Baby, I think I need to remind you of what goes on in this room. First, you called me Warrick. Second, you came without my permission. What am I going to do about that?"

I stepped back again and rubbed my beard, pretending to be deep in thought. My silence made Melanie squirm.

If she wasn't strung up, facing me, I would have spanked her ass until she begged me to allow her to come.

"Sir?" she breathed out questioningly.

"Oh, now you remember my rules?"

I went to unstrap her and carried her to the bed, picking up the spreader bar along the way.

Melanie squealed when I dropped her on the bed and pulled her to the edge by her feet.

I made quick work of getting Melanie's ankles strapped. I then reached over into the bedside table and grabbed a pair of vibrating nipple clamps.

A cry escaped her lips when I clamped her nipples.

"Breathe, baby. Breathe."

Once I felt like Melanie was cool, I lifted her legs high in the air with one hand, and stroked my dick over her clit, spreading her juices between us.

I watched as a bead of precum dripped from the tip of my dick.

That was all I could take. I drove home, plunging deep in Melanie's walls.

"Sirrrrr!" She cried out.

"Yea, baby? You like that? My pussy like that?" I asked.

"Sooo much. I need to come. I feel so full. Can I please come, sir?"

"Good girl."

I thought she was going to forget to ask permission. But I guess the sting on the nipple clamps and my grip on the spreader bar effectively reminded her of where we were.

"Not yet," I told her. "You're not getting off that easily for breaking my rules."

I slowed my strokes, so Melanie could gain some control over her impending orgasm.

She was breaking through her pleasure as if she were in a Lamaze class.

"You learned your lesson?" I asked.

I had her legs wide and high in the air as I continued to

pursue the deep depths of her womanhood. Then I flicked the nipple clamps on low, and Melanie bucked.

"Please, Sir. I promise... I learned my lesson. I will follow your rules–in this room, Sir."

I had to chuckle, because I knew Melanie's ass wasn't prepared to listen to shit I said outside of these four walls.

In response, I smacked Melanie's clit, hard and drove into her.

"Come, Melanie!" I gritted out.

Honestly, she was going to come with or without my command. I felt it. But I didn't want her to think she failed me in any way.

That was a part of being a Dom; I needed to know my submissive fully. I needed to know their body and its limits, and I never wanted to fail Melanie, so I will always be sure to get it right with her.

"Shit, Mel! SHIDDD!"

I couldn't think about anything else any longer. The nut she was pulling from me was taking over every corner of my brain.

Her groans and pants matched my own as we soared over the edge of pleasure.

She was bringing me all the peace I never knew I needed, with just the way she pulled my seed from me. But then, Melanie opened her mouth and solidified it.

"I love you, Sir. So much!"

That was it; my fucking heart exploded. I unlatched her feet from the bar. I needed to feel her against me.

Once I got the bar out of the way, I dropped down and pulled her to me.

"I fucking love you too, Melanie. Thank you for loving me. It's a gift that I will treasure forever." My dick was hardening again, but honestly, I didn't want to be confined to the rules of these four walls at the moment.

I wanted to hear my name falling from her lips.

So, I picked Melanie up, with our bodies still connected, and carried her to my bedroom.

With every step, Melanie bounced on my dick, and we'd both groan from the currents of pleasure traveling through our bodies.

When we were in my room, I headed straight for the shower, and turned the multiple showerheads on high.

"Baby, I'm gonna have to put you down so I can clean you."

"I don't want you to let me go."

"Never, baby. Never."

Melanie sniffled.

"Hey! Don't do that. Don't cry, Mel."

"They're happy tears. I never thought I would find love after years of settling for the bare minimum. Never thought love after heartbreak and failure could feel this good... so full. Thank you for not giving up on me."

"I told you long ago, Melanie—you're mine. I meant that shit then, and I mean it even more now. Now, let me clean you up so I can dirty you up again."

The giggle that escaped Melanie's throat attacked my heart and dick at the same time.

And I couldn't believe that she was willing to deal with my ass. That she really wanted me.

I was finally going to have to accept the fact that someone genuinely loved my broken ass.

Chapter Thirty-Five

MELANIE

I couldn't believe how quiet, and easy life had been for the past eight weeks.

It truly felt like I was floating on a cloud. Warrick has been treating me like the rarest treasure, while still doing the dirtiest things–that I loved–to my body. My life had truly taken a turn for the better, and I was ecstatic.

I even forgave my big-headed ass brother for always meddling in my life.

It was also a weight lifted off my shoulders at the thought of him and Warrick not wanting to kill one another.

Sinaa teased me endlessly about going to be tied up and sexed good every time I mentioned spending time with Warrick.

I knew she was just intrigued by the life.

To my dismay, she even told me about some of the things she talked Malachi into trying out.

I could always tell when they did too, because my brother

would look at Warrick with a level of disgust only a brother could when knowing intimate details about his sister.

I even overheard him telling Warrick to, *tell my sister to stop sharing shit with his wife.*

Warrick cackled and replied, *don't hate.*

Weeks following Warrick and I's reconnection, the family has gotten together to chill quite often.

Naomi and Zinae seemed to like Warrick. And thanks to that damn social media scandal, their asses had even been caught a few times whispering shit. I prayed to the Lord Almighty above that my daughter didn't get any ideas.

Knowing that she was having sex was enough. I did not want to think of her being tied up and spanked.

I'll kill that little boy, Roman! I mused.

Today, everyone was getting together at Malachi's for a cook-out, and I was helping Sinaa with the salads.

"It's nice to have a moment of silence before everything kicks off."

"I agree. It's been so loud lately. With Warrick and Malachi always arguing about football, to the girls always running around with them damn cameras... to them two big ass dogs Malachi got for you... it's always jumping in here."

"I know. You're going to have to get Warrick to start hosting some shit. He has a bigger damn house anyway."

I laughed because Warrick hated people in his personal space.

"I think I could talk him into it."

Sinaa smirked.

"I bet you can... little nasty ass."

I laughed.

"Whatever. Don't hate the player; hate the game."

"You're so damn corny," Sinaa said and rolled her eyes. She headed over to the fridge to pull out a small bottle of apple juice. "You want something to drink?"

"I'll take one of those apple juices."

"What? No tequila and sparkling water?"

"Not today, sis."

I had to clamp my damn lips together to keep the smile from my face.

"Why aren't you drinking?" I countered.

Sinaa looked around the kitchen, making sure one of the girls wasn't going to jump out with a camera.

"I'm pregnant," she whispered.

I squealed, then clamped my hand over my mouth.

"OMG! Yes!" I whispered-shouted. "Congratulations. I'm so happy for y'all."

"Girl, thanks! But I can't believe I'm going to have a kid in college and then pushing one out of my damn coochie. What's wrong with me?!"

I couldn't hold back my laughter. I also couldn't keep the lid closed on my own news any longer.

"We're going to be in the same boat," I whispered.

"I fucking knew it! You haven't drunk any alcohol for the past few weeks. Not even a mimosa during brunch."

"Bitch, you either! I just didn't want to be the first to say anything. And I haven't told Warrick yet. It wasn't planned. It must have happened after I had the flu and all those meds had my hormones all out of whack. And I had just started taking birth control pills, but you know that are less effective."

"Oh goodness. How do you think he's going to take it?"

I shrugged. I really didn't know. I have been hiding it from him for two weeks, and each day I felt guiltier.

"I don't know, but I have to tell him. "

Just then, Warrick and Malachi walked into the kitchen.

Warrick walked up behind my stool and wrapped his large hand around the front of my neck, pulling me to him, and kissing me on the ear.

"Nigga, do you always have to draw attention to that shit?" Malachi said, pointing his finger to where Warrick was playing with my collar.

"Mel, I can't believe you let this nigga tag you like that."

Malachi was still coming around, but some things he couldn't hide his disdain for. And my collar was definitely one of them.

"Didn't I tell you to mind your business, Malachi? I got this over here."

Malachi took in a deep breath and changed the subject.

"Anyway, what y'all in here whispering about?" Malachi asked.

I barely registered his question. All I could think about was how much my honeypot started leaking at Warrick's touch. He nonchalantly applied a little pressure, just the way I liked it.

"Probably about how your sister is pregnant and hiding it from me."

Sinaa and Malachi's mouth dropped open. And I stiffened against Warrick.

"It's okay, baby. I knew before you did. I know everything about your body."

"You're not mad?" I timidly asked.

Warrick leaned down and whispered in my ear.

"Oh, I'm definitely going to punish you for it."

My heart started racing, and I'm sure if I were a few shades lighter, my cheeks would be bright red.

Whew, thanks for that good melanin!

That didn't matter though, because Malachi said, "I don't

want to hear that shit, man. Bad enough I already know about your fuck dungeon, but don't talk about that shit in my house."

That lightened the mood, and we were all laughing except for Malachi.

"Are you okay with having a baby?"

"Never better, Mel. I love you, and if our son or daughter has half the heart and spirit as you—which I know they will—then they're going to be amazing."

"Awww..." Sinaa was all caught up in the moment.

I was too, but I was also thinking about my punishment later.

Warrick continued to stroke along my neck, playing with the collar I wore every day. He was successfully ruining my panties.

"We're going to be new mommies together! I can't wait," Sinaa said. We were all congratulating one another and sharing hugs.

Then we heard a loud thump upstairs.

"Mama!"

"Mommy!"

Both Naomi and Zinae yelled at the same time.

Me, Malachi, and Sinaa looked at one another and burst out laughing.

"I think they found y'all video!" Warrick said and laughed.

We all cackled, trying to school our faces before they stormed the kitchen.

The End

CONNECT WITH SHAY

Facebook: https://bit.ly/376Qynf
Instagram: https://bit.ly/3lUD3gq
Facebook Group: https://bit.ly/3moC5zo
Twitter: https://bit.ly/2UV7qHM
Website: https://shaydavispens.com/
Amazon: https://amzn.to/3fsaUuC

SHAY'S CATALOG

MY FREAKY ALTER EGO – EVA SHERIE

Held In Contempt: An Erotic Novella
Wild Thoughts; Reckless Nights: A Sexy Novella

Made in the USA
Middletown, DE
16 September 2023

38628615R00130